THE STORY OF A LITTLE GIRL WHO
DANCED HER WAY STRAIGHT
TO HER HEART'S DESIRE.

KATRINKA DANCED BAREFOOT DOWN THE VILLAGE STREET

KATRINKA

THE STORY OF A
RUSSIAN CHILD

BY
HELEN EGGLESTON HASKELL

NEW YORK
E. P. DUTTON & CO., INC.
PUBLISHERS

TO
W. E. H.
AN EVER DEARER COMRADE

KATRINKA LIFTED PETER AND WENT STUMBLING THROUGH
THE DRIFTS

CONTENTS

PAGE

A LETTER TO THE ONE WHO READS THE BOOK ix

CHAPTER

I KATRINKA AND PETER 1

II KATRINKA ASKS FOR HELP . . . 10

III AT IVAN DROVSKI'S 23

IV KATRINKA RETURNS HOME . . . 32

V KATRINKA HEARS OF AN ENGAGEMENT 37

VI EASTER MORNING 49

VII THE MESSAGE 60

VIII KATRINKA AND PETER ARE HUNGRY . 67

IX KATRINKA STARTS ON A JOURNEY . 82

X KATRINKA SELLS THE SAMOVAR . . 89

XI KATRINKA MAKES NEW FRIENDS . . 100

XII KATRINKA VISITS THE SCHOOL . . 108

XIII KATRINKA RESUMES HER JOURNEY . 117

XIV THE PROMENADE OF GIRLS 131

XV KATRINKA DANCES FOR THE CZAR . . 142

XVI KATRINKA AND PETER SET OUT AGAIN 149

XVII THE CHILDREN REACH ST. PETERS-
       BURG 155

XVIII STEFAN NORVITCH TELLS A STORY . 166

CONTENTS

CHAPTER   PAGE

XIX   WHEN THE CZAR WAS A BOY . . 175

XX   KATRINKA SEES A PARADE 188

XXI   KATRINKA MAKES A NEW FRIEND . 194

XXII KATRINKA PASSES THE EXAMINATIONS 209

XXIII THE GRAND DUCHESSES VISIT ST.
      PETERSBURG 217

XXIV THE FAVORITE SONG OF THE GRAND
      DUCHESSES 231

XXV   KATRINKA AGAIN SEES THE GRAND
      DUCHESSES 241

XXVI BLESSING THE ORCHARDS 248

XXVII KATRINKA JOINS THE CZAR'S DANCING
      CLASS 254

XXVIII KATRINKA DANCES IN THE FESTIVAL . 266

XXIX KATRINKA ENTERS THE IMPERIAL BAL-
      LET 276

XXX   KATRINKA ATTENDS A BALL AT THE
      WINTER PALACE 283

XXXI KATRINKA APPEARS IN THE IMPERIAL
      BALLET 295

XXXII HER HEART'S DESIRE 312

ILLUSTRATIONS

Katrinka Danced Barefoot down the
Village Street . . . *Frontispiece*

Katrinka Lifted Peter and Went Stumbling
through the Drifts . . . .

"Make Haste and Bring me the Key to
this Box" . . . . . .

Katrinka Was Unaware that a Lady had
Stopped to Watch her . . . .

Her Heart's Desire . . . . .

A LETTER TO THE ONE WHO READS THE BOOK

Dear Schoolmate:

You will probably be very much surprised when I tell you that there are not many Russian immigrants in the United States. I was surprised, too, when I found it out. There are a great many immigrants from Russia, but that is quite a different matter.

Russia is a huge country in which a number of peoples live, more or less unwillingly, under the rule of the Russian Czar. There are the Slavic peoples to whom the Poles and Ruthenians, and the Russians themselves, belong. There are the Teutonic people, the Germans, some of whom live in Russia. There are the Hebrews, whom we call Russian Jews, and whom we usually mean when we speak, in our ignorance, of Russian immigrants; but they are not Russians, and they have nothing to do with this story; perhaps some day they will have a book all their own in our Schoolmate Series, but not this year.

The other people whom we think of as Russian immigrants are the Ruthenians, or as they are sometimes called, the Little Russians, to distinguish them from the real or Great Russians. But the Ruthenians live in Austria-Hungary as well as in Russia, and most of those who emigrate to America come from Austria-Hungary, so it really does not seem quite fair to call them Russians, does it? Still, as a nationality, they are closely related to the Great Russians; cousins, we might call them, and there are about 26,000,000 of them living in Southern Russia, where their chief city, Kiev, was the capital of the country before the founding of Moscow in the middle of the twelfth century.

These Little Russians bring to us Americans the gifts of poetry and song; they are celebrated for their songs of love and war. And even after they come to America they make songs; but alas, they are now songs of the dark mine and the cruel "boss." The Ruthenians are dancers too, as well as poets. Does it not seem hard that we should so often give only poverty and wretchedness to these simple-hearted, trustful strangers who bring us such joyous and beautiful treasures? But out in the Canadian

Northwest, where they can own farms, the Little Russians are happier than in the United States. One of their countrymen, Michael Gowda, has even translated into Little Russian our own Whittier's "Snow-Bound."

The Ruthenians are also a religious people. Some of them belong, like the Great Russians, to the Greek Orthodox Church, and others are called Uniates, and obey the Pope of Rome, who, however, allows their priests to marry and to wear beards, and to recite the prayers and the service in the Slavonic language instead of in Latin. There are many of these Uniate churches in America, and you may know them by their three-barred crosses.

But you must not think that there are no real Russian immigrants in America. There are the Doukhobars, those strange Russian peasants who, about one hundred and fifty years ago, became convinced that Christ forbade all war and fighting, and that it was not necessary for them to follow the rules of the Greek Church in order to worship God.

Of course, this independence of spirit did not suit the Russian Czars, and from 1785 to 1800 hundreds of these poor people were banished to

Siberia, and others were tortured. In the
early years of the nineteenth century they were
given a breathing spell by the Czar Alexander
I, who let them settle on land in Russia just
north of the Crimea reservation, where they
could live according to their ideals of coöpera-
tion and peace; but the Czar Nicholas I broke
up the colony and sent them to the Caucasus.
This was between 1841 and 1845. And then,
unfortunately, they began to quarrel among
themselves, despite their peaceful intentions,
and one faction reported to the Czar's officers
that the other faction "was in rebellion against
the government," so that there was more misery
for them, until it happened that Count Leo
Tolstoy, the greatest Russian of the nineteenth
century, or indeed of any century, heard of
their misfortunes, and in 1898 a petition was
presented to the Czar's mother, the Empress
Dowager, when she was passing through the
Caucasus, and she was asked to plead with her
son that these poor peace-lovers might be allowed to emigrate or to settle in some part of
the Russian Empire where they would not be
tormented.

They were told that they might leave Russia

if they would go before the next annual con-
scription took place; that is, before the next
time for choosing soldiers to serve in the Czar's
army; and through the prompt help of the Society of Friends,—Quakers in England and
America,—they were hurried across the ocean
in four ships to British Columbia, where land
was waiting for them. The Quakers, you see,
had a special sympathy for them, because of
their unwillingness to fight. If there had been
more Doukhobars in Russia, if all the peasants
in Russia, Germany and France, had been willing to die rather than take up arms against one
another, the great war that has ravaged Europe
in 1914 and 1915 could never have been begun.

And besides the Doukhobars in Canada, and
the Ruthenians in the United States, there are
here and there in America, Russian men and
women who have tried to overthrow the despotic government of the Czar, and have had to
flee from their country in haste, for fear of being executed or exiled to Siberia. One of
these, a woman,—and an old woman now,—is
widely loved in the United States. Her name
is Katharine Breshkovskaia, but her friends
call her Babushka,—little grandmother. She

came here a number of years ago, after having served a long term of exile in Siberia. Wherever she went, in America, she made friends who begged her to stay with them, safe away from the spies of the Russian government, who were only waiting an opportunity to put her in prison again. But although she was old and gray, and worn by the hardships of exile, she said she would never cease to work for the freedom of her people as long as her life should last. So her American friends bade her good-by, with tears, and she went back to her dangerous work fearlessly. Of course, it was not long before she was arrested again, cast into prison in Russia and then sent out to Siberia, where she is now,—the beloved Babushka of all the young Russian men and women who suffer to-day in that bleak land for the sake of Russian freedom.

The father and mother of Katrinka, the little dancer in Mrs. Haskell's story, were also sent to Siberia, because they had a printing-press in their house and were trying to teach the village people to read and write. The Russian government is afraid to have its peasants go to school, lest they learn how much better off the people are in other countries. So Katrinka's father and mother were called revolutionists, and were sent away into exile at night, while their little girl and boy were asleep. But Katrinka's story ends more happily than most of the Russian stories of exile. There are not many revolutionists so fortunate as to have a little girl who can dance her way into the presence of the Czar, win fame for herself and pardon for her family.

This Czar, whose picture Mrs. Haskell draws so well, will, perhaps, seem to you a very strange person,—so tender and kind to his own little daughters and little son, so loving to his own wife, and so hard and indifferent to the people outside his own family, even allowing the Cossacks to shoot them down in the streets as if they were dogs. But it is not only in Russia that one finds this kind of man. There are many others like him even in America; men who guard their own little boys and girls from all harm and hardship, but who are quite indifferent to the fact that thousands of other people's children work all day in factories, and are ragged and dirty and hungry and ignorant. No doubt these men would be horrified if they thought they were like the Czar of Russia, for we Americans who have not yet forgotten our own struggle for liberty, do not like to think of ourselves as the oppressors of our fellowmen.

If the Great War brings liberty to the oppressed peoples in Russia, to the Poles and the Jews and all the others; if it teaches the Czar and his nobles the meaning of brotherhood, and brings to the more democratic nations, like England and America, a wider, purer vision of liberty for all people, it will not have been fought in vain.

Affectionately yours,

FLORENCE CONVERSE.

KATRINKA

CHAPTER I

KATRINKA AND PETER

K ATRINKA [1] opened her eyes, blinked
sleepily, then drawing her shawl about her
shoulders, sat up and looked around. Beside
her, Peter, his stiff black hair tousled and his
red lips parted over his tiny teeth, still slept.
Katrinka, shivering, tucked the blanket more
closely about his shoulders. It was unusually
cold, even for Russia. The top of the big oven,
where she and Peter had spent the night, was
barely warm.

Katrinka leaned forward, her eyes on the
two small windows with their tiny panes of
glass. A fine, sandy snow was falling. The
light in the room was gray and cheerless, the
house wrapped in silence. Katrinka felt suddenly lonely and afraid.

1

"Mamusia," [2] she called softly.

There was no answer. She called again, then waited. All was silent. Katrinka bit her under lip, thoughtfully. Usually, when she awakened, her mother was pat-patting around the kitchen getting the tea and black bread ready for breakfast.

Katrinka slipped from the top of the stove and opened the door leading into the other room. It was empty and very cold. She turned back into the kitchen, and going to the broad shelf running along the wall beneath the window, sat down on the edge of it and began rewinding the bandages that she wore in place of stockings.

She had slept in her dress of brown cloth and her crimson blouse, and although she had loosened the bandages on her legs before she had snuggled down beside Peter on top of the oven, she had not removed them. Now, she swiftly took off the long strips of brown cloth, then began to wind one of them about her right foot, beginning at the toes and securing the end of the bandage cleverly under the first swathings. Around and around her ankle and calf she passed the bandage until, presently, her leg in its tightly wound folds looked almost as if it were encased in a heavy stocking. When both legs were neatly covered, she slipped on her funny, sandal-shaped shoes, made from strips of braided bark, with wooden soles.

Then she ran to the door, and opening it just enough to squeeze through without letting in any more cold air than was possible, sped through the snow to the log stable back of the house. This was surrounded by a high fence made of branches thickly woven together to keep out wolves. As she entered the stable, the hens set up a great cackling and gathered around her, expecting to be fed. The cow turned its head and studied her with patient eyes, then mooed as if complaining that it was long past the milking hour.

"Father," called Katrinka, softly at first, and then louder. "Father, where are you? Father! Father!"

At her feet the hens clucked and scratched in the straw. The cow looked at her and again mooed dismally.

"Mother!" There was fear in Katrinka's cry now. "Mother, oh, mother!" Her voice sounded high and shrill. "Mother, Mamusia, where are you?" There was no answer. Again Katrinka called, then with hands clasped on her bosom ran from the stable, stopping at the gate in the fence of wattled branches to look up and down the zigzag village street.

The snow was so fine and thick that she could see only a short distance, the neighboring houses showing like misty, dark patches through the white haze.

In her haste to find her parents she had forgotten to tie over her head the handkerchief-shaped shawl which she always wore when out of doors in winter, and her ears were red from the cold. The frost from her breath gathered in her nostrils and whitened her black lashes and brows. Her teeth began to chatter. Her hands were purple with cold.

"Mother! Father!" Her voice seemed swallowed up by the long white road. In a neighbor's yard a dog yelped.

Suddenly the door of the cottage opened. In it stood little Peter, wailing for his breakfast. He was barefooted. The wadded coat in which he had slept was open in the front, showing his plump, brown breast.

Seeing him, Katrinka, who was about to

start down the village street in quest of her parents, turned back, and running to the house, gathered the little boy up in her arms and carried him into the kitchen. Opening the door of the big clay oven, she set him down inside, then went to the storeroom for birchwood.

The fire was almost out, but Katrinka soon had it blazing cheerily, for she stripped the bark from the birch, as she had often seen her father do, and used it for kindling.

Having started the fire, she turned her attention to bandaging Peter's feet and legs and putting on his bark sandals. Then she lighted a tallow candle, and holding it in front of her, made another trip into the dark storeroom under the house. It was a low room with white-washed walls against which hung the huge sides of several salted codfish. Some hams and a great many strings of small fish that her father had smoked and salted, swung from the beams. All about on the floor stood barrels and jars of salted cucumbers, pork and cabbages.

Going to a shelf, Katrinka found a pan of sour cream and a loaf of black bread. She carried these upstairs and set about getting breakfast for herself and Peter, although she was so full of strange fears that she had little appetite. Never before had her father and mother gone away without saying good-by. Even in the summer, when they had to go a great distance to harvest the crops on their tiny farm, they breakfasted at home.

This morning they had gone without a word of farewell and without having prepared for themselves even a cup of tea before leaving. The big copper samovar [3] stood in the middle of the table, just as Katrinka's mother had left it the night before, its charcoal ready for lighting.

Katrinka filled its reservoir with water, then lighted the charcoal. When the water began to boil she brought Peter and placed him on his high stool. She filled his cup half full of sugar before she poured his tea. Then she spread a slice of break thickly with cold cream and offered it to him. Peter looked at the bread, then shook his head and covered his eyes with his chubby hands.

"Matuska," [4] he sobbed over and over again, using his pet name for his mother.

"Matuska will come by and by," said Katrinka, doing her best to comfort Peter. "She has gone for a walk in the snow. Perhaps, if Peter is good, she will bring him something from the store. I have made the tea as sweet as bees' honey, Peter, and see how thickly I have spread the cream on the bread."

Peter continued to dig his chubby fists into his eyes, shaking his head and wailing dismally, with his mouth wide open.

"Listen, Peter," coaxed Katrinka. "The little man behind the chimney [5] is getting cross. I hear him moving around. If you are not good he will come out and eat up your breakfast." Peter continued to cry. Katrinka laid her arm across his shoulders. "Oh, Peter," she whispered in a tragic voice, "close your mouth. A naughty spirit with fire for hair is sitting on top of the samovar, waiting to fly down your throat. Shut your mouth quickly."

Peter lowered his arms and closed his mouth.

"Where is the naughty spirit?" he demanded, looking eagerly around.

Katrinka laughed. "He flew into the oven when you closed your mouth," she said, a dimple flashing into her cheek. "Eat the nice black bread, Peter, and drink your tea."

She held the cup of sirupy tea to his mouth. He drank it, unwillingly, his eyes wandering from one corner of the room to the other, in search of the fairy with fiery hair.

Meantime Katrinka's great brown eyes were fixed on the gate, which she could see from the window and through which she expected that her father and mother presently would return.

After Peter had finished his breakfast she put on a shawl and, going to the gate, again looked up and down the village street. Then she returned to the house and crossing the kitchen went into the other room where the big loom stood in the middle of the floor, hiding from view the little printing press on which her father wrote in black letters to far away people. All day yesterday her mother had sat at the loom. Katrinka blinked back the tears that threatened to fall as she recalled her mother's head as it bent over the cloth she was weaving, her black hair forming a curly frill around her rosy face.

Katrinka walked around the loom, then stopped with a cry. The little printing press was gone. She ran into the kitchen and seizing Peter in her arms dragged him into the corner of the room farthest from the door. Her eyes were wide open and frightened. Her small face white with fear.

"Somebody has been here, Peter. Somebody has taken away the printing press," she whispered. "And father and mother are gone. Perhaps the Cossacks have been here."

"The Cossacks [6] do not touch good little children," said Peter, patting Katrinka's cheek.

She laughed in spite of herself. "Of course not, Peter. And they have not taken father and mother away, for father and mother were good, and all good folks are safe from the Cossacks."

She looked up, and, as her eyes fell on the picture of the Virgin on the wall, she ran towards it, then, bending her knees, sprang suddenly straight into the air and placed a fleeting kiss on the Virgin's forehead, striking the floor again as lightly as a feather in spite of the clumsiness of her bark and wood sandals.

CHAPTER II

THE snow was almost a foot deep. Little Peter constantly stumbled and fell, so that finally Katrinka lifted him, and, with her eyes fixed on the gray blur which she knew was the house of the nearest neighbor, went stumbling through the drifts. She wore a sheepskin coat, the fur on the inside. A gay, red woolen handkerchief was tied over her head. She had taken off her bark sandals and had slipped on a pair of knee-high leather boots that belonged to her mother. Her feet slipped up and down in them, and as now and then she sank in a drift, they scooped up quantities of snow in their loose tops. This melted, and running down inside, wet the cloth bandages and made her feet and ankles cold. Her eyelashes and brows were white with frost. Even the curls of hair that clung about her forehead as they escaped from the woolen head wrapping were frosted.

Peter was crying softly for his mother.   His tears froze on his round cheeks and hung from his chin in tiny icicles.   Katrinka was too cold and heartsick to try to pacify him.   For seven hours she had waited for her parents to return and at last, despairing, was on her way to the house of Ivan Drovski to ask advice.

When she set out, the house looked like a far-away gray blur through the veil of snow; but as she stumbled on, the blur took shape until at last she could distinguish a single window in the front of it and a low door with the snow piled high against it.

"See, Peter," she cried, her eyes fixed on the friendly shelter, "we are almost at the house of Ivan Drovski.   Dry your eyes, we shall soon have news of mother."

She staggered through the gate and set Peter down for a moment, to get breath enough to go on.   While she waited a face appeared at the window, another joined it and another, until presently six pairs of eyes were peering through the tiny panes at Katrinka and Peter. Then, suddenly, the low door at the side of the house opened and Ivan Drovski, big and bearded, wrapped in his great sheepskin coat,

kicked away the snow and came striding down
the path towards the exhausted children.

"Why, Katrinka, my little lamb, what brings
you out in such a storm?   Is the good mother
or father ill?"

His voice rumbled like a bass drum.   He
tossed little Peter to his shoulder and taking
Katrinka by the hand, started towards the
house.

At the door he set Peter down, for he was so
tall he had to bend almost double to avoid striking the beam in the top of the doorway.   After
he had crossed the threshold he reached back
for Peter, placing him in the crook of his elbow
and holding out a hand for Katrinka.

It seemed to Katrinka, who was blinded by
the snow, that the room they entered was as
dark as night, and she stumbled and would have
fallen had she not struck a warm, furry body
that she knew belonged to a young calf which
lived in the cottage with Ivan Drovski and his
family.   As she righted herself there was a
great whirring and fluttering of wings above
her head, made by the pigeons that built their
nest among the rafters in the outer room of the
Drovski cottage.   She was wading through

straw to her ankles but the air was warm and felt grateful to her half-frozen face.

Clinging to Ivan Drovski's great hand she made her way through the darkness, almost stumbling over the hens and chickens scratching in the straw and a little family of sleeping pigs that set up a shrill squealing which delighted Peter.

Presently Ivan Drovski opened another door, a trifle higher than the one which had admitted them to the outer room, and entered the kitchen, which was lighted by the small window through which six pairs of curious eyes had watched Katrinka and Peter.

A large woman with a broad good-natured face stood in front of the whitewashed clay oven, which was set in the wall so that it heated both the kitchen and the outer room. As Ivan threw open the door she hurried to meet him, taking Peter from his arms and unfastening his wadded coat while she questioned Katrinka.

"What has brought you out in such a storm, my child?" she asked, shaking Peter's coat vigorously over the oven.

"Mother and father have gone away. They

have been gone since early morning and Peter
and I are very much afraid."

Mother Drovski stopped shaking Peter's
coat and stood looking at Katrinka with her
mouth open. Three small children clung to
her skirts, staring shyly.

"What do you mean, child?" demanded
Ivan, shaking himself like a bear and unfastening Katrinka's coat. "Have your parents
gone for a visit?"

"I do not know," said Katrinka, her lips
quivering. "They were there last night.
There was a meeting. Some strange men and
women talked. Peter went to sleep in his
basket.[7] Then mother put him to bed on the
oven and told me to lie down beside him. They
closed the door to the other room. By and by
somebody rapped and then there was more talking. Father and mother did not come to bed
with us on the oven and this morning I could
not find them. The cow has not been milked
although I fed her with straw. Peter and I
have waited all day for father and mother.
When it began to grow dark I was afraid.
The printing press is gone."

"Ah," breathed Ivan Drovski, as his thick

brows puckered into a frown, "the printing press is gone, is it?   I warned your father that it would make trouble for him.   Now it has come.   Who knows when we shall see him again?"

Ivan thrust his fingers through his long yellow beard.

"My poor lambs, what will become of you?" cried Mother Drovski, gathering the children into her arms, while her own family huddled in the corner under the image of the Virgin and crossed themselves, frightened at the anxious note in their mother's voice.

Katrinka, who had kept her tears back all day, felt her eyes fill as Mother Drovski's arms closed about her.

"Is it the Cossacks who have taken them away?" she asked, her voice smothered against her kind neighbor's shoulder.

"I saw strangers in town last night," rumbled Ivan.   "They stopped at the store for tea.   Somebody said they were secret police from St. Petersburg.   Now our good neighbor and his wife are gone.   That is what comes of learning reading and writing, and holding meetings."   He shook his head dolefully. "They will find a grave in Siberia while their children starve."

Katrinka tore herself from the sheltering arms of Mother Drovski and looked despairingly into the face of Ivan. At last she understood what was meant by the disappearance of her parents. The police had taken them away. Even now they were on their way to that mysterious place called Siberia of which she had heard so much. Many of her father's friends had gone there. She had heard often, how, chained to one another, they had crossed the frozen desert, never again to come back, but to spend their lives working far under the ground in the Siberian gold mines.

There flashed through her mind a picture of her mother's face as she had seen it on the last Easter, her cheeks rosy. her dimples flashing. She had worn a dress of vivid blue, the color of the corn flowers, and her hair was confined under a lace handkerchief. Around her waist was tied a wonderful apron made of strips of crocheted lace and white linen. Her full plaited skirt was short and gave one a glimpse of her ankles bandaged in white cloth and of her slippers of black leather, the only leather slippers in all the village. How gayly she had laughed as she stopped to exchange kisses and Easter eggs with all whom she met!

Katrinka felt her chin quiver. Could it be that she should never again see the pretty, sweet-voiced mother of whom she had been so proud, the mother who had sat at home spinning while the other women in the village went to the fields to be hitched beside the oxen or the horses at the plows?

The tears rolled down Katrinka's cheeks. She hid her face in Mother Drovski's apron.

"Do not worry, my little one," said Mother Drovski, laying her arm about the child's shoulders. "You and Peter shall not go hungry. Your stomachs shall be filled and you shall sleep with us—here in the izba [8] of Ivan Drovski—with him and his own little ones. It has been a hard winter. The cattle are suffering for food but with the help of the good Father we shall find enough for two more mouths."

Mother Drovski crossed herself with her thumb and two first fingers, her eyes on the pictured face of the Virgin framed in a wreath of tin flowers that hung in a corner of the kitchen.

"Dry your tears.   We will light the samovar and have tea at once."

She motioned to a tall girl, who immediately set to work preparing the big samovar which stood in the middle of the pine table.   Then, turning to Katrinka, she went on kindly.

"Come, we will go down cellar."

She took Katrinka's hand and drew her to the door that led into the storeroom under the house.   At the head of the stairway she stopped to light a candle while Katrinka bravely blinked back her tears.

"We will have some beet-root soup with slices of cucumber in it," she said as they reached the foot of the stairs.   "And there is a loaf of black bread in the oven."   She paused and bent over the potato bin.   By the light of the candle Katrinka could see that it was almost empty.   For some moments Mother Drovski stood looking into it, then, with a sigh, she filled a wooden bowl with potatoes.   "They will not last through the month, but you shall have some to-night," said the good woman.

trying to speak cheerfully. After filling the bowl, she held up the candle and looked around the storeroom. Katrinka looked too, her brown eyes wide and filled with wonder. The room was less than half the size of the storeroom at home. Against its walls hung no strings of dried and salted fish. There were no jars of preserved berries on the shelves. A single barrel of salted meat stood on the floor. Mother Drovski shook her head sadly, then, going to a jar that stood in the corner, uncovered it and took out a single cucumber. Near the jar was a box filled with beets and turnips.

The flickering candle lighted up Mother Drovski's troubled face. She was wondering if the scanty supply of winter provisions would be sufficient to feed two more mouths.

Katrinka, seeming to read the good woman's thoughts, caught her rosy underlip between her teeth. She looked around dubiously at the bare storeroom, her mind conjuring up a picture of the storeroom at home with its supply of good things, and of the kitchen with hams, sides of bacon, strings of mushrooms and dried fruits hanging from the rafters.

Suddenly she clapped her hands. Her feet

in their big boots, wet with snow water, felt
light. She sprang into the air and coming
down whirled around on her toes. It was
Katrinka's way to express her feelings through
her feet, which were like thistledown, and very
small.

"Oh, Mother Drovski," she cried, "Peter and
I will eat with you to-night and then you and
Ivan and the children shall come home with us
and stay until father and mother come back.
We have a big house and there are hams and
fish and potatoes and cabbages enough to feed
the whole village."

As she finished speaking she felt a moment's
misgiving over the generosity of her invitation.
She was not sure that her father would be
pleased to come home and find Ivan Drovski
and his family installed in the house, which
was the largest and lightest, as well as the
cleanest, in the entire village.

She wondered if the Drovskis would bring
the chickens and the calf and the little pigs to
live in the sitting room and if they would scat-
ter straw over the shining floor. Appalled by
the picture she laid her forefinger against her
lip, shrinking into the shadows for fear kind

Mother Drovski would read her thoughts.

That good woman breathed a sigh of relief. "I have heard of the riches of your father," she said. "Surely it would be but right for us to take a few dried fish and some barley meal in return for the care of his children. And, Katrinka," she continued, starting towards the stairs, "is there an abundance of straw in your stable?"

"I heard father say that it would last until spring. Do you need some straw?"

"Ivan began pulling straw from the roof to feed the cattle two days ago. But if we use up the entire thatch there will not be straw enough to last until the snow is gone," replied Mother Drovski as she bent to close the cask in which the pickled cucumbers were kept. "I am sure your father would willingly allow us a little straw to pay us for sheltering his children."

"But, Mother Drovski, you are to live with us. Our house is large and there is room in it for all of us. Besides, if Peter and I come here to live with you, there would be nobody left at home to water the geraniums and to milk the cow, and keep the fire burning."

Mother Drovski patted Katrinka's head, dripping a splash of hot tallow on the child's upturned face as she did so.

"We will leave those questions until later," she said, moving towards the stairs.

CHAPTER III

IT was a restless night that Katrinka spent in the overcrowded izba of Ivan Drovski. Although she was accustomed to sleeping on top of the big oven at home during the long winter nights, with little Peter's head on her arm and her mother and father occupying the space beyond Peter, it was impossible for her to sleep on the Drovski oven, upon which was huddled the entire family, with the exception of Ivan, who slept on the shelf under the window.

In order to make room for all, Peter and the youngest Drovskis were laid crosswise at the foot of the oven against the wall. Katrinka and two half grown girls occupied the middle space, flanked by Mother Drovski and Marie, the oldest daughter.

The room was so hot and stifling that Katrinka's sleep was broken, and again and again

23

she opened her eyes, fixing them on the gray square of light made by the window, wondering if morning would ever come. Her position was cramped and uncomfortable, but she dared not change it for fear of disturbing the kind neighbors who had so willingly taken Peter and herself into their already overcrowded house.

With the first gleam of daylight she slipped to the floor and pulled on the leather boots that belonged to her mother. After a night in the oven these were thoroughly dry, although as hard as stones. Making as little noise as possible Katrinka groped her way to the other room, crossed it without disturbing either the pigs or the hens, and opened the door into the yard. The snow had stopped falling. The morning was crisp and clear. She took a deep breath of fresh air and plunged into the great, white drift of snow that had piled up against the door during the night. Her eyes were fixed on the house at the end of the village street. Suddenly she felt a hand on her shoulder.

"Where are you going, my child?" rumbled Ivan Drovski.

"I thought I would run home while Peter slept to find out if father and mother had returned and to give the cow some straw."

Ivan Drovski wound the full skirts of his sheepskin around him and shook his head.

"Go back into the house, little one. I will look after the cow and bring you news of your parents, if there is any."

He opened the door of the outer room where the calf and the little family of pigs were already bestirring themselves. "Breakfast will be ready in a few minutes and Peter will be crying for you."

Reluctantly Katrinka turned her back on the snow-covered landscape and waded again through the drift to the dark little izba of Ivan Drovski.

Entering the kitchen she found Mother Drovski beating up some pancakes, while Marie, the oldest daughter, wrapped in a wadded coat and carrying a pail on her arm, was about to start for the spring back of the house.

"Fill your pail with snow, Marie," said Mother Drovski, "the spring will be frozen over and the ice too thick for you to break.

Besides, snow water makes good tea and the snow melts more quickly than ice. But make haste, the little ones are already stirring." Marie started towards the door and Mother Drovski turned to Katrinka. "You may set the table, my child. We must have breakfast ready by the time Ivan gets back with the milk."

Katrinka set the table and when Marie returned with her pail full of snow, she emptied it into the reservoir of the samovar and lighted the charcoal. Meantime she planned how she should manage to return with Peter to their own clean and spacious house without wounding the feelings of Mother Drovski, who was already treating them as if they were her own little ones.

The water in the samovar had just begun to boil when Ivan Drovski returned with a bucket full of warm milk.

Katrinka ran to meet him. "Were mother and father at home?" she cried.

Ivan Drovski shook his head, then, as he saw the tears spring to her eyes, laid one of his great hands on her shoulder.

"Do not cry, my child. I will go to the vil-

lage to-day and learn what I can concerning
the whereabouts of your father and mother.
Meantime you and Peter shall not suffer.   You
shall make your home with us."

She bravely blinked back her tears, but when
breakfast was over and Ivan leaned back in his
chair, sipping his tea through a big lump of
sugar which he held between his teeth, she
slipped from the table and going to his side,
laid her hands on his arm.

"Now that Peter and I have finished breakfast, Ivan Drovski," she said with a wistful
smile, "we will go home.   Father and mother
would be frightened if they should come back
and find us gone.   It is best that we wait for
them there."

"Poor lamb," said Ivan, crunching his sugar.
"There is no use in your going home to wait
for your parents.   You will be lucky if you
ever hear from them again, much less see them.
Best stay content with us.   The izba is warm
and when we have moved the provisions from
your storeroom to ours, there will be plenty of
food for all."

Katrinka compressed her lips.   "I thank
you, Ivan Drovski," she said, "but I must take

Peter and go home. There is nobody else to water the geraniums and keep the fire going in the oven so that the kitchen will be warm when father and mother come back."

She released Ivan Drovski's arm and taking Peter's wadded coat from a hook on the wall, wrapped it about him.

"Come, come, my child," said Mother Drovski. "Be sensible. Your father and mother are half way to Siberia by now. Make up your mind to remain comfortably with us. We are willing to care for you and Peter until you can take care of yourselves. You are a smart girl and can make yourself useful."

"No, Mother Drovski," said Katrinka stubbornly, "I thank you, but Peter and I must go home. My mother has taught me how to make a good soup and to bake black bread. I am ten years old and almost as tall as Marie, who is fifteen. I can knit and mend. I will go home and write a letter to the Czar, asking him to send back my father and mother."

Ivan Drovski's big laugh rumbled through the room.

"Many another child has written to the Czar, the Little Father, as they call him, and for their pains more than one has felt the knout and the Cossack's whip.   Come, my child, and rest with us."

Katrinka looked at Ivan and shook her head, biting her rosy under lip to keep back a homesick sob.

"No, Ivan, I will write to the Czar and I will pray."

Again Ivan laughed.   "Write to the Czar, if you will, then, but remember what Ivan Drovski tells you.   It will do no good.   Your letter will never find the Czar—you will be lucky if it comes under the eyes of one of the Grand Dukes."

With the words Ivan rose, thrust his arms into his sheepskin coat and strode towards the door.

Katrinka took Peter by the hand and started to follow him.

"Wait a minute, little ones," called Mother Drovski.   "If you are determined to go home, I will go with you."

She long had wanted to see the storeroom of her neighbor, Peter Petrovski.   Rumor said that it was provided with good things enough to feed the entire village until spring.   She remembered how last year, during the famine, Peter Petrovski had kept his neighbors from starving by dividing his stores with them.

She pinned a shawl over her head, wrapped another around her shoulders, thrust her feet into huge boots and strode towards the door. Her children started after her but she waved them back, and with Peter on one side and Katrinka on the other, went through the dark room where the hens clucked and scratched in the straw and the little pigs fought over their food.

She stopped for a moment to pat the young calf which brushed her cheek with its rough tongue, then passed through the low door into the fresh outdoor air.

Peter blinked and covered his eyes with his hands. After the dark interior of the house the sun on the snow blinded him. Katrinka took long breaths of the cold air. The blood danced through her veins. She broke away from Mother Drovski's restraining hands and went leaping and skipping through the snow, her large boots flapping up and down.

She threw back her head, waving her arms towards the sky. She skimmed nimbly over a snow-covered rock at the side of the road, plunging in and out of the drifts, then, her cheeks glowing, her lips parted, ran back to her neighbor.   For a moment her joy in movement had caused her to forget the disappearance of her father and mother.

CHAPTER IV

KATRINKA RETURNS HOME

EVEN the cold and empty izba did not depress the buoyancy of Katrinka's spirits. At once she set about building the fire, singing softly under her breath, gayly confident that before another day was over her parents would be restored to her. While she laid the birch wood, Mother Drovski looked about the kitchen, shrugging her shoulders at the spotlessness of the floor and at the glistening whiteness of the big oven. In front of the little window stood a stand spread with a snowy cloth. On this were several geraniums in full bloom. Above the stove hung shining copper kettles and stew pans. The samovar that occupied the middle of the rough table in the center of the room was so bright that she could see her face in it. The bench that ran along the wall under the window was spotlessly clean.

"It is easy enough to keep one's kitchen like this when there are but two little ones," Mother Drovski muttered under her breath, balancing in her palm a ham that hung from the ceiling. "Your father has enough smoked meat for an army of Cossacks," she went on aloud, with a sidelong glance at Katrinka, who was watering the geraniums. "That is because he has never given to the church like the rest of us and he has only a few mouths to feed."

"And also he works harder than anybody in the village," replied Katrinka.

Then, fearing that she had hurt the feelings of her neighbor, she impulsively moved a bench into the middle of the room and springing upon it reached up and took down the largest of the hams.

"Take this home with you, Mother Drovski," she said, cordially. "I am sure father would want to do something in return for your kindness to little Peter and me."

Mother Drovski put the ham down on the bench and went to the sink where she studied the trough made from a hollowed block of wood. In this trough Katrinka's mother did her washing, and in it she frequently bathed little Peter, instead of steaming him in the oven, according to the village custom.

"They tell me that your mother washes your clothes every week in the winter, just as in summer," said Mother Drovski, running her hand around the smooth inside surface of the trough.

"Yes," said Katrinka, slipping some mushrooms from the long string that hung over the oven and placing them on the bench beside the ham.

Mother Drovski shrugged her shoulders. She washed regularly every week during the summer, carrying the clothes to the river and rubbing them between two stones. But in the winter it was difficult to get enough water for the tea and the steam baths, so like the other villagers she baked the family wearing apparel on Saturday, even the great sheepskin coat of Ivan Drovski going into the oven with the other clothing.

After her survey of the kitchen was finished Mother Drovski visited the sitting room, where she looked at the big loom, the glass case in which stood the sacred images, and some pussy willows that had been saved from Palm

Sunday a year ago, when, as is the custom, they were carried to church instead of palm leaves.

Her big, black eyes saw everything—the white lace tidies on the tables, the artificial flowers stuck in the sand that was poured between the double windows to keep out the cold, the braided mat on the floor, the porcelain stove that had come from St. Petersburg.

This stove was cold now, for the fire that had crackled in it during the meeting, two nights before, had long since gone out, and the room was so chilled that a frost rim began forming about Mother Drovski's mouth. With a shiver she hurried back to the kitchen and lighting a candle went into the storeroom. Presently Katrinka joined her, loading her with salt fish, potatoes, cabbages and beets. In fact it was all that the good Ivan Drovski and his wife could do to carry home in their arms the good things that Katrinka bestowed upon them, as she recalled with a pang of pity the empty storeroom in the Drovski house and the many mouths that her neighbors had to feed.

"We will send Marie to spend the night with you," cried Mother Drovski, when she found that it was impossible to persuade Katrinka to return with her. "She is a big girl, old enough for marriage. With her here you will not be afraid and we shall have more room on the oven at home."

Katrinka smiled. With the sun shining on the snow it did not seem to her that she would ever again be afraid of anything. But when darkness fell and little Peter cried for his mother, and through the stillness she heard the great wolf hounds howling in the village dooryards, she was glad enough that Marie Drovski had come to spend the night, although Marie told harrowing fairy tales of bad spirits that dwelt in the barnyards and amused themselves cutting off horses' tails, and of others that hid in dark storerooms, creeping out by candlelight to tangle the skeins and spoil the spinning. In truth, it is quite certain that when night came, Katrinka would have preferred spending it packed on top of the oven with the entire Drovski family, to passing it alone with Peter in their own clean and roomy izba.

CHAPTER V

SPRING had come. All about the birds were twittering, crocuses and daisies were coming into bloom. The little buds on the lilac bushes had turned green. Katrinka danced barefoot down the village street towards the store, there to exchange dried fish for sugar and tea.

Now and then a shadow swept her brow and her feet grew heavy. This was when she remembered with a pang that no word had yet come from her father and mother. But when spring is in the air and one is only ten years old, tragedy must look on at a distance, while joy sends the blood bounding through the veins. So, on the whole, Katrinka was happy, although she fell on her knees many times a day to pray to the Virgin for the return of her parents, and she had stripped the storeroom of good things until it was as empty as the storeroom of Ivan Drovski, to make gifts to the village priest, in return for his prayers for the happiness of her poor father and mother.

To-day the air was wonderfully sweet and full of life, and Katrinka felt sure that the prayers would soon be answered. Her feet seemed hardly to touch the ground as she approached the store and then suddenly paused. She had almost bumped into Marie Drovski. She laughed, then sprang back to look admiringly at her friend.

Usually Marie wore an old crimson skirt, figured with bright yellow cornucopias, but to-day she had changed it for a skirt and kerchief of dark blue, which in Russia is the mourning color and is always worn by engaged girls— and Marie Drovski had been engaged for almost two months now.

It had come about in this way. A big man driving a fine sleigh had come to the village from the other side of St. Petersburg. He was in search of a bride for his son. He stopped at all the village houses to get a sly peep at the girls of marriageable age. He came finally to the dwelling of Ivan Drovski. As he entered the kitchen he saw Marie, who was taking a big loaf of bread from the oven. It was a white loaf and very light, made from flour that Katrinka had given Mother Drovski the day before. At the sight of the fine white loaf the man struck his hands together delightedly, and asked to see Mother Drovski. After some talk and laughter the visitor managed to find out a great many things about Marie that pleased him. He learned that she could spin, knit, sew, cook, milk the cow and work in the fields. Also he saw that she had a pretty face and guessed that her disposition was merry. He found that when she married she would have as a dower the fine young calf that had been kept in the outer room during the winter, as well as a pig, a sheep and a great deal of cloth that she had spun on the big loom which belonged to Katrinka's mother.

When the stranger learned all this he was very much pleased. He invited Mother Drovski to drive to his home with him, there to inspect a fine jewel that he had. Mother Drovski set out the following day, and that night Marie confided to Katrinka that the jewel her mother was to see was the son of the stranger.

Two days later Mother Drovski returned, well satisfied with the young man whom she had met.

A fine feast was then prepared by the Drovskis, and on the day of the feast, towards evening, three knocks sounded upon the outer door. By this time the snow had almost disappeared and the weather was so much warmer that the chickens, the calf and the young pigs had been taken to the shed back of the house, and the outer room had been cleaned from floor to ceiling. The shutters had been removed from the double windows and the room was light and fairly cheerful.

When Mother Drovski heard the mysterious rapping she pretended to be very much surprised, and going to the door, threw it open. Twilight had fallen and she held in her hand a tallow candle. Two women stood outside.

"What brings you to my dwelling at this hour?" demanded Mother Drovski, as if she did not know who the strangers were nor why they had come.

"We are hungry. We would eat," replied the taller of the women.

"Then enter," said Mother Drovski. "Our

supper is spread.   It is plain and poor but there
is enough for all." Really it was the very
finest supper that Mother Drovski had ever
prepared.

The women lowered their heads and passed
through the outer room into the kitchen.   The
big oven had been freshly white-washed, and
the rough pine table, covered with a white cloth,
was groaning under the weight of good things
to eat.   Marie in her red skirt made a pretty
picture, standing shyly with downcast eyes in
the corner near the glistening oven.   She
knew perfectly well why the women had come.
One of them was the mother of the young man
whom Marie had never seen, but whom her
parents had decided she should marry, provid-
ing his mother thought well of her.

The mother of the young man, a broad-
shouldered woman with sharp blue eyes, looked
around the room, making believe, meantime,
that she had not noticed the girl in the corner.
Untying the white kerchief from her head, she
placed it on the bench under the window.

"I have a son," she said, her eyes fixed on
the face of Mother Drovski.   "He is broad-
shouldered and as strong as an ox.   His face

is so handsome and his disposition so kind that all the girls in our village desire him for a husband. But he will have none of them. He has heard that in this village, in this very house, there is a maiden of sixteen years with eyes as soft as a young lamb's and with a complexion like the sunny side of an apple. It is said of her that she has many virtues; that she goes to church regularly, that she is quick and neat, that she can sew, spin, weave, knit and bake a loaf that is good enough for the Imperial Prince. I have also heard that she is as good as a man in the fields. If there is in this house this beautiful maiden, pray show her to me at once, that I may return and tell my son that I have found for him a fitting bride."

"Indeed," replied Mother Drovski, "I will show my daughter to you. But I fear you will be disappointed. She is a simple village girl, but she works hard and is kind and obedient."

"Pray, let us behold her," said the sharp-eyed visitor, seating herself on the bench that ran along the kitchen wall.

Madame Drovski sighed, and going to the door leading from the kitchen into the back-yard, called softly. Immediately several village girls appeared. They entered the house and one after another passed before the mother of the young man, who shook her head sadly, and after the last girl had gone, turned to Mother Drovski.

"I have made a mistake," she said, picking up her kerchief as if about to leave. "None of these is the girl for whom I am in search."

Then, suddenly, as if she had just remembered her, Mother Drovski called Marie, who came shyly from the corner and stood before the two strange women. Immediately the mother of the young man threw out her arms and gathered the girl to her bosom, kissing her first on one cheek and then on the other.

"This—this is the girl for whom I came in search. This is the maiden for whom my son longs."

Mother Drovski who, according to Russian custom, had planned the whole thing at the time she visited the home of the young man, immediately began to wail and wring her hands. Marie joined in the weeping, and even Katrinka, who had been invited to the feast, managed to squeeze out a few tears, although she knew that both Mother Drovski and Marie had been looking forward to the visit of the unknown young man's mother and were pleased at the prospect of the coming marriage. It seemed very foolish to her for them all to cry aloud now as if they were torn with anguish, but she knew it was customary and so, with an effort, joined in the lamentations.

After a few minutes the tears were dried and the Drovski family, the two strange women, Katrinka and little Peter crowded around the table where the feasting continued for hours.

The next day Marie was driven to the house of a relative in a nearby village where the youth she was to marry had also come. Here the two young people were allowed to see each other but not to speak. The young man, as if ignorant of Marie's presence in the house, strolled about the yard while Marie observed him through a window. Later Marie went outside and stood talking with a cousin while the young man watched her.

It is probable that he was very much pleased with the choice his parents had made, for when Marie at last drove away with her father, he stood for some time in the middle of the road looking after the departing wagon.

All this had taken place some weeks ago, but to-day for the first time Marie had put on her betrothal mourning. To Katrinka's fond eyes her friend looked more enchanting than ever before.

"Oh, Marie," she cried, her gaze fixed on the blue skirt. "You have on your mourning." Then it is true that everything has been arranged for the wedding?"

Marie's color brightened. "Yes, I shall be busy from now on, spinning cloth to make my wedding clothes."

"And in the summer will you go away?" Katrinka's dimples vanished. The corners of her mouth drooped.

"Yes, before the harvesting I shall go to live in the house of my father-in-law."

"Oh, Marie, what will Peter and I do without you? Who will sleep in the house with us after that?" Katrinka bit her under lip to hide its quivering. "We shall be very lonely and afraid, Marie."

"Perhaps your father and mother will have

returned by then," said Marie, smiling cheerfully. "Besides, Peter is getting large and strong. He is four years old. He will soon be a man and able to take care of you."

Katrinka clasped her hands, and the dried fish which she was to exchange for sugar and tea fell unheeded to the ground.

"Oh, Marie, I pray to the Virgin every night that Peter may grow up a woman. I fear that if he is a man he will be a man of the sword and a printer. Then he will be torn from me and sent to Siberia. Even now he plays that he is a soldier and one day he had a stone that he said was a bomb. When I asked him what he would do with it, he said he was going to blow up the Czar's Cossacks. I do not know where he learned about these things, but I am sure it would be better for him if he could grow up a woman."

Marie laughed. "Children hear and remember everything. No doubt Peter heard them talking of these things at the meetings which were held in your house."

"They were all good men and good women who came to our house. They were talking and thinking always of what would be best for the poor."

"That may be, but it is foolish to talk of such things. It can do no good, and if the officers of the Czar hear of it they are very likely to throw one into prison. Have you finished coloring your Easter eggs?"

Katrinka picked up her fish and the shadow disappeared from her forehead.

"I have a basket of them and one for Peter. We have some of every color, but the prettiest are the green ones on which I have painted red flowers. I will show them to you to-night."

Marie smiled and started on her way, then suddenly turned and came back.

"A cousin is coming to eat with us to-morrow. I told my mother that I would bring her some white flour that we might have a nice loaf for him. But when I looked for the flour in your house this morning there seemed to be none there."

"I gave the last of it to the priest yesterday."

"And the codfish is all gone."

"Yes, your mother took a strip—all that was left—when I gave her the last of the cucumbers, Saturday. There are seven mouths to feed in your family. In our house there are only two. Peter and I like black bread and mushroom soup, and there are enough mushrooms to last for a long time."

Marie looked at Katrinka and frowned, shaking her head dubiously.

"You have given too much to your neighbors and the church. You forget that your father is no longer here to provide food for the long winters."

"But Peter and I are very small. We have enough for a long time to come," replied Katrinka, entering the door of the store and offering her fish to the proprietor.

CHAPTER VI

EASTER MORNING

IT was three o'clock Easter morning. Katrinka, who had been taught to cook by her
mother, had made a huge cake the day before
and had covered it with icing. She had sold
some eggs and with the money had bought
some red and yellow paper flowers. With
these she had adorned the top of the cake. Although it would not be dawn for several hours
she and Peter were on their way to church
with the cake, which Katrinka carried on a
great platter. In the moonlight she could see
that the village street was thronged with
women, who like herself, were carrying flower-
trimmed cakes, tower-shaped cheeses and
loaves of bread to church in order that the
priest might bless the first food eaten after the
Lenten fast. One woman had a cake that was
built up in terraces. It was surmounted with a
pink candle and was so heavy that the woman

staggered beneath its weight. As Katrinka overtook the woman and saw the pink candle, she sighed.

Her mother had always trimmed the Easter cake and cheeses with little candles, but after Katrinka had bought sugar and flour and raisins and paper flowers for her cake the egg money had given out, so for the first time the Easter cake was without candles.

All of the day before Katrinka had been busy preparing for the great feast. She had swept and cleaned the house and had set a bowl of yellow daisies in the middle of the kitchen table. Before going to bed she had given Peter a thorough steaming, having first built up a very hot fire in the stove, upon which she afterwards dashed a good sized basin of water. The water steamed and sizzled on the hot surface, filling the kitchen with warm vapor. When the steam was so thick that even the walls were damp, Katrinka took Peter, who was already undressed and prancing about the room, and laid him on the shelf in front of the oven. Then she rubbed him with a rough towel of homespun until he glowed. Finally, she filled the trough in the kitchen with cold water and rolled him in it, afterwards beating him lightly with birch branches until he was as red as her own petticoat.

This morning he was dressed in a little suit of yellow linen that his mother had made for him the summer before. It was a trifle tight and uncomfortable, but Katrinka thought it looked very fine indeed as he ran back and forth in the dim light, swinging a small basket of colored eggs.

By the time they reached the church Katrinka's arms were aching and she was very glad to set her big cake down on one side of the aisle, placing Peter's basket of eggs beside it. This done she took from a capacious pocket in her skirt a little packet of tea, some sugar and two small rolls. These she set on the floor beside Peter's basket. Then she stood up and looked around. The entire church was filled with food. There were cakes and fruit and meal and eggs and butter. In the midst of the good things the white-haired priest moved about with a bowl of holy water.

As he approached her cakes, Katrinka threw out her arms, crying, "Holy Father, bestow your blessing on my sweet loaf. Sprinkle it with one drop of the holy water that it may be blessed."

The priest dipped his hands into the water and then lifted them, shaking the glistening drops in all directions. Katrinka kept her eyes on her food and seeing that none of the water had fallen on the rolls, cried out again, beseeching the priest to return and sprinkle the bread. At last when she was sure that all of her food had been blessed by contact with the holy water, she and Peter gathered it up and started towards home. They were very hungry for they had fasted for seven weeks, and according to the custom of the Greek church, had eaten almost nothing during the seven days before Easter.[10]

Although the sun was not yet up when they entered the house, Katrinka made tea from the package that had been blessed and cut two large slices of cake. Then, having partly satisfied their hunger, she and Peter lay down on the shelf that ran along the wall of the sitting-room and were presently fast asleep.

It was long after sunrise when they again awakened. Fearful that they would be late for the morning service Katrinka hurriedly

brushed Peter's black hair and sent him out-
doors to play while she made her toilet. This
finished, she called her brother.

"How do I look, Peter?" she asked, standing in the doorway, her hands on her hips and
her head tilted to one side, eager for the small
man's praise. She had discovered a few
weeks before what seemed to her a very wonderful head-dress. It had belonged to her
mother when she was a girl and had lived in
the North with her parents. It was a red
turban with an embroidered border. Katrinka had saved it for the Easter festival.
Now with the head-piece rearing itself boldly
above her brow she felt suddenly timid and
sought Peter's approval before starting for
church. The high turban was so different
from the flat kerchiefs worn by the villagers
that she was half afraid to appear in their
midst, wearing it.

Peter looked at it, then began to shout.
"You are a soldier! You are a soldier!" he
cried, leaping up and down and swinging a
stick. "Take your sword and come with me
to fight the Czar's Cossacks."

"Ssh!" said Katrinka, taking off the turban.

"Some one will hear you and then you will be carried away to prison."

"I am not afraid," cried Peter, flashing back and forth and slashing about with his stick. "When I am a man I shall go to war and when the Cossacks have all run away I will pull the Czar off his throne and make him give us back our father and mother."

"Peter," remonstrated Katrinka, looking about nervously, "the Czar will give us back our father and mother when he knows how good they were and how loyal. Come!" She tied her plain white kerchief over her head, smoothed down the full plaits of her bright red skirt that stood out like a hoop around her knees, fastened a white daisy in her bodice, and with a regretful backward glance at the scarlet head-dress which she had abandoned, took Peter's hand and set off towards the church. They had not gone far when a family that lived in one of the neighboring izbas saw them, and came running pell-mell to meet them. Katrinka, who had been walking sedately, dropped Peter's hand and with a little cry skimmed over the grass towards her neighbors. Then began a great smacking of cheeks, for each member in the large family kissed both Katrinka and Peter, and Katrinka and Peter kissed each one of them in return, at the same time exchanging Easter eggs with them. The exchanging of eggs and kisses completed, they all proceeded decorously on their way. But every now and then they came across other villagers, all of whom exchanged embraces with Katrinka, Peter and their companions. At the church everybody seemed to be embracing and kissing everybody else.

Peter and Katrinka laughingly joined in the festival, running about and eagerly smacking grown-ups and children alike.

The appearance of a carriage drawn by three black horses interrupted the merrymaking. The horses drew up with a clatter in front of the church and a strange man with fair hair and hollow cheeks, who had been half reclining in the rattle-trap vehicle, stepped out, and leaning on a staff that he carried, stood staring, half wistfully, at the group of merry villagers in front of the church. Presently Ivan Drovski strode up to the stranger and kissed him heartily on the cheek.

"Happy Easter, friend," he said, and then

turned to the villagers. "Salute the stranger,"
he called out in his huge, rumbling voice. The
throngs crowded around the man, but only a
few ventured to place the Easter kiss on his
cheek.

The stranger smiled sadly at the apparent
reluctance of the villagers to give him the
usual Easter greeting. Then he looked up at
the church, but did not cross himself. Instead,
he removed his fur turban and held up his
hand.

The crowd drew back. There was something
terrifying about this stranger with the fair
hair, cadaverous eyes and unsmiling lips. Katrinka gathered Peter to her side and muttered
prayers under her breath. But in spite of herself, she was fascinated by the new arrival and
could not take her eyes from him. He threw
back his head. His throat was full and white.
Katrinka saw that in spite of his gauntness he
was not an old man. There was something
young and full of fire in his attitude. He
looked around, his eyes resting for a moment
on the face of each one of the silent crowd
Then he spoke.

"I am looking for the children of Peter Petrovski," he said, and his voice sounded like a deep bell. Katrinka cowered behind Mother Drovski.

For some seconds there was silence. Then Ivan Drovski spoke.

"Peter Petrovski's children are here. Have you news for them?"

The stranger thrust his hand under his belted coat and drew out a paper. "Show me the children," he said, his eyes again sweeping over the crowd.

Mother Drovski pushed Katrinka forward and the man saw the child fully for the first time. He smiled. The smile lighted up his face and Katrinka, no longer afraid, went to him, and as he stooped to look into her eyes, she kissed him on the cheek. He smiled again and laid his hand on her head.

"I bring news from your father and mother, little one," he said, speaking so low that even Ivan Drovski, who stood nearby, could not hear his words. "They came to Siberia over the new railroad. They were prisoners, but not in chains. They are well and asked me to tell you to be of good cheer. They are with you always in the spirit. Here is a letter your father gave to me."

He placed a folded paper in Katrinka's hands. She unfolded it, but the tears had filled her eyes and she was unable to distinguish the words that were written on it. The man leaned down and pointing at the lines with his finger, read:—

BELOVED KATRINKA:

Take the tin box in the closet and go to Stefan Norvitch in St. Petersburg. Tell him that you are the daughter of Peter Petrovski. Ask him to open the box and do with its contents what he will, first removing enough to educate little Peter, and to bring you, my beloved Katrinka, to young womanhood. Keep your heart filled with courage and join your mother and father in praying that we may soon be reunited.

Your mother sends a heart full of love and many kisses to her children. Be a brave girl and do not forget

Your loving father,
PETER PETROVSKI.

When the man had finished reading he gave the paper to Katrinka, who placed it in the bosom of her dress.

As the man turned to reënter the carriage, Katrinka reached forward and took his hand, striving to detain him. Gently he withdrew his fingers from her clasp.

"I must go about my business, little one. If God wills I will return in good time and go with you and your brother to find Stefan Norvitch in St. Petersburg."

He climbed into the carriage and, as the three horses galloped away, looked back, smiled, and waved his hand. Katrinka never forgot the expression on his face as the carriage swept down the road, the great bell that swung in the bow over the dashing middle horse, pealing merrily.

CHAPTER VII

AFTER the man had departed Ivan Drovski took Katrinka to one side, waving away the villagers who had gathered about the child.

"What message from Peter Petrovski and his good wife?" he asked.

"My father sent me a letter," replied Katrinka, her eyes sparkling. "He is well and not in chains. He says that Peter and I are to go to St. Petersburg."

"Why, my child," exclaimed Ivan under his breath, "what could two children do in St. Petersburg? Such talk is foolishness." The good man's brow knotted in a frown.

"I do not know, but I must obey my father," replied Katrinka. "He has written."

"We will show the letter to the priest after the service," said Ivan, holding out his great hand. "He will tell us what to do."

Katrinka gave the letter to Ivan Drovski and

then, taking Peter by the hand, went into the church where the Easter services were being held, all of the people standing up or lying face downward on the floor. It seemed as if her father and mother were nearer by than they had been for a long time.

After the service Ivan waited for the priest, and showed him the letter that had been brought to Katrinka by the stranger.

The priest took it, his brows knotted, and when he had finished reading it, thrust it into the pocket of his cassock.

Katrinka looked at him appealingly. She wanted the letter from her father but was afraid to ask for it. She followed the priest as he crossed the little stretch of ground which separated his tiny izba from the church and, just before he stooped to enter his low doorway, called out softly:—

"Father, you have forgotten to return my letter."

The priest turned and looked at the child. He was still frowning.

"No, little one, I have not forgotten. The letter will be returned to you in due time. Go home now, and pray the good Lord that he will keep you from mingling with evil men and women."

The child made a reverence, turned, and slowly walked away.

The priest shook his head, then stooped and entered the low door of his cottage. That very afternoon he dispatched the letter to an officer in St. Petersburg.

On the following Thursday a tall, black-bearded man rapped on Katrinka's door.

She saw him from the window, and the magnificence of his uniform with its golden eagles frightened her, as did his sharp black eyes and the white teeth that glistened behind his black beard.

Nevertheless, she opened the door as wide as it would go and invited him to enter, politely asking him if he would have some tea. He shook his head. He did not take the trouble to remove his hat, which Katrinka thought strange in a man who seemed so rich and intelligent.

"Is this the cottage of Peter Petrovski?" he demanded.

Katrinka nodded shyly.

"I have been sent here by one of the Grand

Dukes. You have in your possession, I am told, a black box. Bring it to me."

Katrinka's knees trembled beneath her. This must be Stefan Norvitch, whom her father had told her to find in St. Petersburg. She looked up at the man fearfully. When she finally summoned courage enough to speak her voice was tremulous.

"Is your name Stefan Norvitch?"

The man frowned.

Katrinka shrank from him. She was very much frightened.

"I am an officer in the employ of the Emperor. I have been sent to demand the tin box which is in your keeping and which you were ordered to take to Stefan Norvitch, the revolutionist. Bring me the box at once, child, or show me where it is hidden."

Katrinka opened the door of the closet back of the clay oven.

"There it is," she said, pointing to a tin box on the shelf. "I do not know what it contains."

The man took the box from its resting place. It was shallow and only about eight inches square, but apparently it was heavy. He

smiled, showing his great white teeth. Then
he tried to open the box and, finding that it was
locked, attempted to pry up the cover. But the
lock was too strong.

"Where is the key to this box?" he asked,
turning to Katrinka.

"I do not know. I have never seen it," the
child replied, shrinking from the man, who
scowled fiercely at her as he pulled from his
pocket a bunch of keys attached to a gold chain.

He tried to fit several keys into the lock without success, then turned again to Katrinka.

"We are wasting time. Make haste and
bring me the key to this box."

"I have never seen it, sir," she insisted. "I
do not know what the box contains. Father
told me to take it to Stefan Norvitch in St.
Petersburg. If you are not he I cannot let
you have the box."

The man shrugged his shoulders, and with
the box in his hand, went out to the carriage
with the three horses and its padded coachman.
The harness shone and the carriage was much
newer and more beautiful than the one that had
brought the stranger to the church on Easter
morning.

The officer who rode in it was plump and red-cheeked. But as it rattled away he did not look back as the man had done who had brought the message to Katrinka from her father. Katrinka sighed as she looked after the carriage and then smiled. After all it was better to have lost the tin box than to have found that this man was Stefan Norvitch, to whom her father had told her to go in St. Petersburg. She felt sure that this stranger who claimed to have come from a Grand Duke would be very cruel to little children.

She laughed softly under her breath. How lucky it was that he had driven off without seeing little Peter, whom he might have carried away!

Relieved at the thought of Peter's safety, Katrinka began to sing, and then, as if she could express her happiness in no other way, went dancing across the meadows, her hands waving above her head, her small feet beating time to her song. At the end of the field she saw little Peter half hidden by the cow that had been turned out to graze on the tender spring grass. She called him to her and, taking his hand went to the house of Ivan Drov-

ski. Ivan and Mother Drovski were in the
fields hard at work with their spring plowing,
but Marie sat on a bench in front of the cottage, sewing lace to the edge of her wedding
petticoat.

Katrinka sat down on the grass at Marie's
feet, and drawing Peter down into her lap,
told her friend of the visit of the magnificent
officer who had driven away with her father's
tin box.

CHAPTER VIII

KATRINKA stood in the middle of the storeroom and looked around. The walls were bare, the casks that had held salted meat, pickled cucumbers and cabbages were empty. She had given the last of the honey to Mother Drovski for Marie's wedding feast. Katrinka shook her head sadly and went to the cupboard where her mother had kept the preserved cherries and strawberries and the delicious bottled grape juice. The cupboard was now bare.

Katrinka sighed. The light of the flickering candle showed that her cheeks had lost their rosy color and that there were hollows in them. The white kerchief crossed over her breast revealed the thinness of her sweet throat.

Katrinka ran her fingers over the dusty shelves, hoping that unexpectedly she would come upon a dried herring. She disturbed a couple of big beetles which rustled away to hide in a crack in the shelf, but there were no herrings.

With a shake of the head and a quivering under lip, she left the cupboard and going to the big stone jars standing on the floor of the storeroom, peered into them. There was a sharp stick on top of one. She took it and stirred the brine in the bottom of the jar where the cucumbers had been kept. Then with another sigh she turned to the stairway.

"Peter will cry if there is nothing but berries and a crust of the black bread," she said under her breath. "I will go out and hunt again for some mushrooms."

She blew out her candle and, tying her kerchief over her head, went to the pasture. Her feet lagged. She felt very tired. In the distance the cow, which had given no milk for a month, was contentedly chewing her cud. Katrinka looked at her reproachfully, then as her eyes fell on the ground, laughed gleefully. Almost at her feet were two beautiful mushrooms nestled, half hidden in the grass. She pulled them up carefully, and laying them in a large leaf, hid them in a corner of the fence.

Cheered by her good fortune, she called to Peter to come and help her look for others. The child came trotting dutifully toward her. He was wearing the yellow frock in which Katrinka had dressed him on Easter morning and which had fitted so snugly. Now, although Easter had long since passed and the dress should have been tighter than ever, it hung quite loosely upon him. For Peter, like Katrinka, was very thin. There were blue hollows under his cheek bones, and his little nose looked sharp and pinched.

Katrinka's breath caught in her throat as she looked at him. Then her eyes wandered in the direction of Ivan Drovski's cottage. At Ivan's there was milk and plenty of sour, black bread. But Marie's wedding was to take place Sunday and Mother Drovski was busy preparing for the feasting that would last for three days. Katrinka looked longingly towards the cottage, then shook her head and resumed her search for mushrooms. She and Peter would be in the way. Besides, the Drovskis' store-room would be as bare as their own by the time Marie's wedding was over, and there were many mouths to be fed in the Drovski izba.

Poor Katrinka!

She felt faint. Her feet no longer skimmed the ground as lightly as thistledown. There was a strange feeling of hollowness under her breastbone and her head ached. For two days there had been only a few crusts of black bread in the house and these Peter had eaten. Mother Drovski had given her milk, ever since the cow had gone dry, but yesterday when Katrinka had gone for it she had been given only a part of the usual allowance, because the big cheeses for the wedding would take all of the milk that the Drovski cow gave.

"My own babies will have to get along on cabbage soup and bread for the next few days," Mother Drovski had said, shaking her head sadly as she looked at Katrinka, "and so will you and Peter. But after the wedding—well, as I have told you before—there is always room in our house for Peter Petrovski's little ones, and you will soon be big enough to work in the fields with the women."

Katrinka had thanked Mother Drovski and had gone slowly home. She felt that she could not again ask for milk. Half-heartedly she searched the field and the neighboring roadside for mushrooms and berries, then went to the straw-thatched stable in search of eggs. But there were only two hens now, and she found no eggs.

Inside the cottage the big samovar still stood in the center of the pine table. But it had not been used for many days. There was neither tea nor sugar in the cupboard, and after to-day there would be no bread, not even a crust.

Katrinka fried her mushrooms in oil that her mother had made from the seeds of sunflowers, looked over the few berries she had gathered, arranged them nicely in a yellow bowl and lifted Peter to his high stool.

Peter tasted the berries, then pushed them away.

"Peter wants bread and milk," he said crossly.

"First eat some mushrooms and the nice, red berries, then, by and by, Katrinka will give Peter some bread and milk."

Peter shook his head obstinately, but after some coaxing Katrinka prevailed upon him to eat the mushrooms and berries. When he had finished these he again asked for milk and set up a loud wailing when Katrinka told him that he must wait until night, when Ivan Drovski had finished milking.

Katrinka's dinner consisted solely of wild berries, and when she had finished this meager repast, she felt weaker than ever. But she kept up a brave front for Peter's sake.

She washed her dishes, tidied her little kitchen and whitewashed the stove. Then with Peter she started down the long village street towards the house of the white-haired priest. She had given many a strip of bacon, many a fine ham, as well as potatoes and flour, to the priest during the past six months. Now she was going to ask him to give her food enough to keep her and little Peter from starving during the next few weeks.

The old priest was working in his garden and, as Katrinka approached, smiled a friendly greeting.

"And what has the lamb for an offering to-day?" he asked as she drew near.

"I have not come with an offering to-day, Father. I have come to ask alms. Peter is hungry. Our cow has gone dry. Our hens do not lay any eggs. The garden which Ivan Drovski has plowed and planted for us will yield nothing for some weeks. We are hungry and Peter cries for milk."

The priest's face grew serious. "And you have come to the church for aid? Oh, my child, these are hard times for the church and for the good Czar, the head of it. As for me, I have a large family of my own to feed and my storeroom is almost empty. You should be giving alms, not asking them."

"But, Father, I have nothing more to give and Peter is starving."

The priest looked at Katrinka, scowling.

"How does it happen that with all the riches left in your house when your father and mother went away, you have come to such straits that you ask aid of the church?" he demanded sternly. "What have you done with the fish and pork, the bin full of potatoes, the cabbages, the beets, the cucumbers? Surely two children have not eaten everything."

"Oh, no," said Katrinka. "The winter was long. Many of our neighbors needed food. My father always helped those poorer than himself, so I did what he would have had me do. I gave to the hungry whatever they asked. Surely I did right."

"So that is the way the wind blows! Well, then, my child, since you have come to me for help and advice I will give it to you."

Katrinka's head suddenly stopped aching. The color flashed into her cheeks.

"Thank you, Father," she said, making a reverence and seizing the priest's hand in order to kiss his finger tips. The priest patted her head, smiling into her upturned face. "Yes, child, I will help you. Go to the neighbors whom you helped in their need, and ask them to help you, now, in yours. Tell them that I sent you."

"But, Father, they are no better off than they were last winter. They were hungry then. They are still hungry. I cannot ask help from them."

"Tell them that I sent you. Surely there is enough food in the village to keep two orphaned little ones from starving."

Tears rose and filled Katrinka's eyes as she looked at the broad back of the priest, which he had turned towards her as he finished speaking. She brushed them away, then her gaze wandered to the windows of his small house where his wife sat sewing.   The woman looked pale and ill.

Katrinka smiled at her as cheerily as she could.   She felt sorry for the priest's wife, because in Russia, although the people love the church, they shun the priest and his family. Neither the children of the peasants nor the children of the nobles associate with the priest's children.   It is considered very bad luck to come upon him unexpectedly in the street.   If his wife dies he must give up his parish, take leave of his children and enter a monastery, because a priest without a wife is not allowed to live in a parish, and a second marriage is forbidden.

His oldest son must become a priest, no matter how unwilling he may be, and his daughters must marry priests.   Frequently they never see their future husbands before the wedding ceremony.   Pictures and descriptions of these girls are sent to all the church schools in the country. When a young man has completed his education for the priesthood he writes to the father of the girl whose picture and description have pleased him, and a marriage is arranged.   The wedding must take place before he is given a parish in order to fulfill the law of the Russian church, which provides that no unmarried man can be a priest.

The priest's wife smiled and nodded at Katrinka and no doubt would have gladly asked her to tea, if she had not felt certain that the child would have refused such an invitation, as the villagers deem it unlucky to eat or drink in the house of a priest.

As Katrinka again turned her face towards the street, the tears once more rose and filled her eyes. She walked slowly with down-drooping head. House after house she passed, pausing now and then to look wistfully into the open doorways. There was scarcely a family which had not benefited from her generosity during the past winter. But something—either pride or shyness—kept her now from asking alms. No, there must be some other way. Her knees trembled as she climbed the slight rise of ground which led to Ivan Drovski's cottage. Peter was waiting for her near the gate. As Katrinka looked at him she knew that Mother Drovski had given him some milk. The front of his jacket was wet with it. Marie sat on a bench in front of the house putting the last stitches into her full skirt. Her hips burst like shelves from her tight belt.

The Drovskis had fared well since Peter Petrovski had been taken away. Ivan Drovski had come every morning to milk the cow for Katrinka and to bring in an armful or two of birch wood for the fire, while Marie had slept in the house with the children every night since the disappearance of Katrinka's parents. In return, longing to show her gratitude for their kindness, Katrinka had loaded her neighbors with provisions, and the Drovski children had grown fat and rosy as they had never been before.

But now that the provisions had given out she could no longer repay Ivan for taking care of the cow and bringing in the wood. She had given him the last of the salt fish the day he had plowed the garden. Katrinka sighed, then threw up her head courageously and smiled at Marie.

"Thank you for giving Peter a cup of milk, Marie," she called. "He is growing so fast that he is always hungry." She paused, then went on, making a brave attempt to seem cheerful.

"I found a lace and linen apron in mother's chest yesterday. I will send it to you to-night by your father when he comes to feed the cow. I am sure it will become you."

Marie showed all of her pretty teeth in the smile she flashed at Katrinka.

"Thank you," she cried, and then bent again over her work.

Katrinka took Peter by the hand. They were a long time in reaching home, although it was but a little way, for Katrinka's feet dragged. When, at last, she reached the house she sank down weakly on the doorstep, her chin in her palms. She knew that the time had come when she and Peter must have help from the outside, but it was the first of June and the whole village seemed poverty-stricken. Last year's provisions were exhausted and this season's crops were not yet ready.

Presently Katrinka's thoughts were disturbed by the plaintive mooing of the cow. Ivan Drovski had assured her that in a few days there would be plenty of milk again. Katrinka smiled wanly. By that time she and Peter would have starved to death. She rose wearily, called Peter, and undressing him, put him to bed on the shelf under the window, although it was still early in the afternoon. If he went to sleep now, she reasoned, he would not miss his supper.

Katrinka lay down beside her brother, her dark eyes wide open, resting first on one piece of furniture, then on another. Suddenly a wonderful idea came to her, and forgetting her weakness, and the heavy feeling in her head, she sprang to her feet, and as of old danced across the floor, waving her thin, little arms above her head. In front of the table she paused.

On it stood the shining samovar. She gazed at it, her eyes glowing. Then, in spite of her hunger, she began to sing, choosing one of the songs the young men in the village always sing before starting away to join the army. Afterwards she blew a kiss towards the samovar, whirled around, opened the door and went outside. As she walked towards the enclosure that her father had made for the chickens, the old weakness returned, but she still hummed softly. She looked at the two fat hens that were scratching in the dirt, then started down the road towards Ivan Drovski's house. Halfway there she met Ivan coming up the slope.

"Good evening, my lamb," he shouted. "I was on my way to your house."

Katrinka smiled. "And I was in search of you, Ivan Drovski. Our hens do not lay. I will bake one and give the other to you." As she spoke a shadow clouded her brow, for the hens seemed like old friends, although they laid no eggs.

"I will lose no time," replied Ivan, his face lighting up. "But first I will take a look at the cow."

He went around to the back of the house, and then began shouting to Katrinka.

"Come, child. Here is a present for you. Come quickly, and call Peter."

Katrinka made haste to join Ivan, who was standing in the door of the stable. "Come here, little one," he shouted.

She entered the low stable door and saw lying in the straw on the floor beside the cow, a tiny, baby calf. She cried out in delight, clasping her hands. Then the thought came to her that there was another mouth to be fed and she sighed despairingly.

"In a few days you will have milk to spare," cried Ivan, running his hand gently along the cow's back. "And now I will see about the hens."

Ten minutes later a fine plump hen, picked and dressed, was placed on the kitchen table.

Katrinka threw wood on the fire, and before the sun went down, the cottage was filled with pleasant odors. Peter danced gleefully back and forth patting his small stomach in delighted anticipation of the approaching feast.

CHAPTER IX

KATRINKA STARTS ON A JOURNEY

IT was just daylight on the following morning that two children passed the house of Ivan Drovski. A sack made from a strong linen sheet was swung over the back of the older child, a girl of ten or eleven. She had knotted the four corners of the sheet securely and she held the ends firmly in her two hands. The sack was heavy and the child walked with bent back to ease its weight. Beside her a boy danced gayly, running off now and then into the fields to look for flowers and mushrooms. He found an abundance of flowers but it was not until they had passed the church at the end of the village street that he picked his first mushroom.

"Look, Katrinka," he cried, running towards the girl, who had stopped breathless at the top of the hill. "I have found a pink mushroom."

The girl smiled. "It is very pretty, Peter,"

she said; "you shall eat it with salt for your dinner."

"And the leg of the chicken? You said you were saving that for my dinner to-day. I am hungry, Katrinka; it is time for dinner now."

The girl laughed. "No, Peter, we must travel a long, long distance before we eat dinner. Come, the sun will be up in a few minutes and all of the village will be out. We must hurry or somebody will see us and then we shall be scolded for beginning our journey without first discussing it with our neighbors."

She drew the sack higher over her shoulder and started briskly down the incline. A little feeling of fear and desolation was already taking possession of her, and in order to keep up her sinking spirits she began to talk gayly.

"We are going to St. Petersburg, where the streets are all beautiful and the houses are made of marble and gold," she said. She had never seen a great city except in her dreams.

"All of the people there are merry. They laugh and sing and the Little Father goes about among them showering blessings on their heads. And nobody is hungry. When we get there we will go to the Little Father and ask him to take us to Stefan Norvitch."

"Why do you say 'Little Father,' Katrinka? Father is bigger than Ivan Drovski."

"The Little Father is the Czar. He has five children, one of them a little boy only two years older than you."

"Will he play with me, Katrinka?"

"Perhaps, if you are good."

"What is his name?"

"Alexis."

"Has he a yellow jacket like mine?"

"He has many jackets of different colors."

"Has he a sword?"

"Yes, although he is only six years old. He is an officer of many regiments."

"So am I," cried Peter, "and I have a sword. Tell me some more."

"Wait until we reach the bazaar,[11] Peter."

"When will that be?"

"In a little while. It is in the next town."

"Is the next town St. Petersburg?"

"Oh, no. This town is only eight miles from our village. St. Petersburg is much farther. Before we reach St. Petersburg we come to the town called Tsarskoe Seloe [12] where the Czar and his children live."

"Will they let us sleep in their oven?"

"They do not sleep on the oven, Peter."

Peter pouted. "Do they sleep on shelves? I like the oven better."

"They sleep on beds that are as soft and warm as fur. But see, there in the field is a brown mushroom." Katrinka laughed. "We shall find more than we can eat."

Peter gathered the mushroom and a short distance farther on the children came to a place where the road divided. Katrinka stopped.

Two roads now stretched before her. She did not know which one led to the town where she had heard there was a bazaar to which people came from far and near to buy and sell things. While she stood hesitating, a man driving a shaggy little farm horse approached. Katrinka drew Peter into the grass at the side of the road and held up her hand.

The man brought his horse to a sudden halt, and leaning from his wagon asked if he could give her a lift.

"No, I thank you. We are on our way to St. Petersburg. But first we want to stop at the village of Tosna, where there is a bazaar. Which of these two roads goes there, please?"

The man laughed. "So you and the little one are going to the bazaar. It is a long journey by foot. Take the road to the right. If I overtake you on my way back, I will give you a ride. What have you in the sack?"

"I am taking our samovar to the bazaar to sell."

"Well, good luck," said the man, and crossed himself. It was not unusual in the spring for Russian peasants to be obliged to part with their most treasured household possessions. The winters were long and hard. It was easy to see that Katrinka had gone hungry more than once. The wagon rattled down the road. The children stood looking wistfully after it until it disappeared, then resumed their journey.

At ten o'clock they sat down by the roadside and Katrinka untied the great sack and took from it a tiny bundle which she opened and from which she produced the leg and back of the chicken.

She gave the leg to Peter, who bit into it ravenously. The chicken was tough, for Katrinka had long ago given away the young pullets, either to the priest or to her needy neighbors, keeping two old hens until the last. She had felt a fondness for them because they had raised families the year before. But, to the children, the tough meat tasted delicious and they picked the bones until not a shred of meat remained. Then Peter set his teeth into the pink mushroom, offering the brown one to Katrinka. This she refused, urging Peter to eat it himself, and sprinkling salt between its feathery gills. She was afraid that Peter would be hungry again long before they reached the bazaar.

After they had finished their luncheon she threw the heavy sack over her shoulder. Then she and Peter again started on their journey. The sun beat down upon them pitilessly, for summer comes suddenly in Russia, intense heat frequently following severe cold. But they went on courageously until, by and by, Peter's feet began to drag. Now and then he stopped and, sitting down by the side of the road, begged Katrinka to take him home. By one o'clock both children were very hungry again, but there was nothing for them to eat excepting a few sunflower seeds that Katrinka had been saving to plant.

On every side of them they saw men and women working in the fields and gardens, the women weeding the cucumber beds on their hands and knees, or, hitched beside cows, dragging the heavy plows. Their bright skirts and kerchiefs made pretty patches of color, and Katrinka longed to abandon her weary pilgrimage and stop and talk with them. Only her desire to reach the bazaar before dark stopped her.

To brace her waning spirits she sang the village war songs and hummed tunes that Ivan Drovski played on his accordeon.

After a while the sun went down and the air grew cold. Peter said he wanted his sheepskin coat, but it had been left behind. Then he insisted on returning and made Katrinka's progress difficult by tugging at her skirts and beseeching her to go back.

Too tired to remonstrate with the child, with back aching and hands stiff and sore from holding the pack, she went stubbornly on, and just as darkness fell her perseverance was rewarded. She saw in the distance the lights of the village of Tosna.

CHAPTER X

TAKING heart Katrinka struggled forward, pointing to the lights and telling Peter that presently his stomach would be filled with good things. She began to sing again, choosing Peter's favorite songs. Her voice was sweet and true, although it quavered now and then and sank away for want of breath.

Suddenly there was a great pounding of hoofs behind the children. Turning her head Katrinka saw almost upon them a carriage drawn by three black horses, their skins glistening, the chains on their harness clinking and the bell in the wooden arch above the middle horse ringing merrily.

Frightened, Katrinka drew Peter to the side of the road. As she did so she accidentally let go of the corner of the sheet which held the samovar. It slipped from her shoulder. The samovar rolled almost under the horses' hoofs.

With a cry Katrinka sprang forward to save
it, while the driver pulled up his horses so suddenly that, for a moment, they were almost on
their haunches, their forefeet waving wildly in
the air.

"What is it?" cried a child's shrill voice, just
as Katrinka dragged her pack safely to the side
of the road, and a man jumped from the carriage and stood looking down at her. In one
terrified glance Katrinka recognized him. He
was the officer who had carried away the tin
box. Thrusting Peter behind her, she faced
him defiantly, sure that this time he would demand the samovar and perhaps her little
brother as well.

The man looked at Katrinka, scowled darkly,
and muttering something under his breath,
turned towards the carriage. Katrinka was
uncertain whether or not he had recognized her.

"Are the little ones hurt? Did the horses
strike them?" asked somebody in the carriage.
Katrinka looked beyond the man towards the
speaker.

In the half darkness she saw a little girl with
a sparkling, rosy face, framed in fair, curling
hair on which was jauntily perched a full, black

velvet Tam o' Shanter. Her coat was also of black velvet and was finished at the neck with a wide, lace collar. Her hands were encased in gloves and her feet in shining, black shoes. Katrinka looked at her and smiled shyly. The child smiled back. Then she turned to a woman sitting beside her, said something, and when the woman nodded, leaned from the carriage.

"Did the horses strike you?" she asked.

Katrinka shook her head. "No, and the samovar is safe."

"Your samovar?" inquired the woman who sat beside the child. "What are you doing out here in the road with a samovar?"

"I am taking it to the bazaar," replied Katrinka, once more throwing the pack over her shoulder.

As she almost doubled under its weight, the child spoke to her again.

"It is heavy—have you walked far with it?"

"From our house in the village of Vachok."

"But that is a long way from here!" cried the woman, who spoke strangely and very slowly, as if she were trying to think of the right words.

"It is nine miles from Tosna," replied Katrinka.

"And you have carried the samovar all the way. How tired you must be! We will drive you the rest of your journey. There is plenty of room. Fraülein will hold the little boy. We drive through Tosna on our way to Tsarskoe Seloe." As the little girl in black velvet finished speaking, she turned to the lady beside her, who shrugged her shoulders as if annoyed, and said something in a language that Katrinka could not understand. Whatever it was, it made no difference to the child's plans. She leaned forward, asked the driver to take Katrinka's pack, then motioned to the dark man in the handsome uniform to help the children.

He bowed politely to the child, muttered something under his breath and the next moment had tossed little Peter into the carriage. Poor Katrinka, very much frightened at this sudden turn in events, and still fearful that the dark man wanted to get possession of the samovar and of Peter as well, hesitated, then clambered into the carriage and sat down beside the little girl with the velvet coat.

A fur-lined rug was thrown over them, a

signal given to the driver and the carriage whirled away, the bell over the middle horse ringing, the chains on the harness clashing musically. The air against Katrinka's face was cold, but exhilarating.

She turned and smiled at the little girl in the velvet Tam o' Shanter. As the girl smiled back, Katrinka noticed a roguish expression in her eyes. She did not seem a bit afraid of the big, dark man.

Katrinka pointed to him. "Is the officer your father?" she asked.

The child laughed. "No, indeed," she said. Then she laughed again and spoke in a strange language to the woman on the other side of her.

"My name is Tatiana Nicholovna," she said, turning towards Katrinka. "Have you never heard of me?"

Katrinka shook her head. "I live far from here," she explained apologetically. "I know only the villagers in Vachok."

Again the girl laughed, and just then the horses drew up before the bazaar. The shop-keepers were beginning to close their booths, but as the carriage approached, they stopped,

faced about and stood with uncovered heads.
The next moment Katrinka was lifted to the
ground and Peter was standing beside her. In
her hands was the sheet in which rested the
samovar.

Tatiana called a merry good-by, the lady beside her nodded and smiled slightly, the officer raised his hat without glancing at the children. Then the horses thundered away.

Katrinka gazed wistfully after the departing
carriage, wondering if she should ever again
see the little girl called Tatiana Nicholovna.

Her thoughts were rudely interrupted by
several shopkeepers who crowded about her,
gesticulating excitedly and asking questions
about the Grand Duchess Tatiana and Tsarskoe
Seloe.

It was with some difficulty that Katrinka
explained to them that she had something to
sell, opened the sheet and displayed the
samovar. Then began a whispered consultation accompanied by many gestures. The men
looked at the samovar, passing it back and forth
among them. Finally a thin little man with
shrewd eyes detached himself from the others,

and approaching Katrinka, asked if she would accept a rouble [13] for the machine.

Before the child had time to reply one of the other men told her he would give two roubles. This seemed to Katrinka a great deal of money, and she was about to say that it was too much, when the first man said he would give three roubles. Somebody grasped his arm and there was another consultation. Then the man who had offered three roubles again approached Katrinka.

"Will you take two roubles for the samovar?" he said.

Katrinka looked at him, surprised that he should now offer but two roubles, when a minute before he had said that he would give three. For a moment she stood looking helplessly from one to another of the men. Then she nodded her head.

"It is very kind of you to say you will give me two roubles," she said.

The man placed two roubles in her palm. As her fingers closed on the coins she felt very rich, indeed. She took Peter's hand and was starting towards the street, when she noticed a woman in one of the booths who was putting away a string of dried fish. Going to her she held out the money she had just received.

"Will you please let me have some fish and tell me where I can buy some milk and black bread for my little brother?"

The woman smiled kindly at the children. "You little ones who drive with Grand Duchesses, what do you want with black bread?" she asked, shaking her head.

"We are hungry," replied Katrinka simply.

"Then come home with me. I will give you food and send you back to your mother with full stomachs."

Katrinka's lips quivered. "My mother and father are far away, but they are not in chains."

The woman laid her hand on the child's head. "Do you come from far?" she asked kindly.

"Yes, from Vachok."

"Did the Grand Duchess bring you all the way from there in her carriage?"

"Oh, no. We could see the lights of Tosna when the carriage overtook us. I was frightened and dropped the samovar. The horses almost crushed it with their forefeet, but I sprang in front of them and rescued it. Then suddenly the carriage stopped and the little girl asked if I was hurt. Was the lady with the strange way of speaking, the Grand Duchess?"

The woman looked at Katrinka in surprise.

"No, indeed! The child—the little girl— was the Grand Duchess Tatiana Nicholovna."

"She told me that was her name, but she did not say that she was a Grand Duchess."

"Why, child, she is the second daughter of the Czar of Russia. She passes the bazaar often." The woman's voice had sunk to a whisper.

"Oh," cried Katrinka, "if I had known that I should have told her about my poor father and mother. When she learned how lonely Peter and I have been without them, and how hungry, she would have spoken to her father and he would have sent for them to come home. If you will tell me where she lives, I will leave Peter with you and go at once to find her."

The woman laughed and patted Katrinka's shoulder.

"It is a long way to the Little Palace in

Tsarskoe Seloe, where the Czar and his family live. You could not walk the distance in less than three days."

The woman pulled the canvas flap over the front of her little booth, and reached out a hand for each of the children to grasp.

"I live only a few doors farther on. My sister, who lives with me, will have a hot supper ready by the time we arrive. Come, my little ones."

Peter would have preferred remaining to look at all of the wonderful shops. He was especially fascinated by one where parrots and green and yellow canaries were sold.

He hung back, his sleepy gaze fixed on the big cages filled with birds, until suddenly the proprietor came out of the booth and dropped the canvas curtain. Then Peter fixed his attention on a stand where cheeses were sold, and Katrinka, noticing the droop at the corners of his mouth, slipped her fingers from the hand of her new-found friend, and ran to the booth. Opening her small fist, in which she still held the money she had received for the samovar, she asked the man in charge of the booth to give her a cheese, and to take the pay for it from the two roubles in her hand. The man took a rouble, and was giving her a few kopecks [14] in change, when the woman who had befriended the children, and who had hurried after Katrinka, spoke up sharply. Then followed five minutes of haggling over the price of the cheese, and a great many kopecks were poured finally into Katrinka's hand, instead of a few. The purchase concluded, the market woman took the cheese, and together the trio started down the road, the woman talking cheerily about the good things that the children would have for supper.

CHAPTER XI

KATRINKA MAKES NEW FRIENDS

IT turned out that the woman lived in a very comfortable-looking house. It was made of stucco and rubble stone and was painted yellow, while the gable and window sashes were a vivid blue.

To Katrinka's eyes, accustomed to the rough, log izbas which they had in her native village, the house seemed both beautiful and luxurious, and when the door was opened and her eyes beheld a wonderful, tiled oven set in the wall so that it could heat two rooms at a time, finished at the bottom with a shelf wide enough to accommodate a large family, she gasped in delight, while even the tired and hungry little Peter smiled.

The room was delightfully warm and was filled with the odor of good things. A table, laid with a white cloth, stood by the window and on it a samovar bubbled merrily. A woman in a full, brown skirt and a white apron was just taking a hot loaf from the oven, as the door opened. She called out a cheery greeting without looking around. When she had placed the loaf on a snowy piece of linen, she turned and a wave of surprise swept her stolid face as she saw the children.

"Sister Elizabeth, I have brought two little pilgrims home with me," cried the market woman, lifting Peter from the floor. "They are hungry, having walked all the way from the village of Vachok. I have asked them to spend the night with us. In the morning they can resume their journey to St. Petersburg."

"But what will two such mites do in that great city?" demanded Sister Elizabeth in a deep but pleasant voice.

"Our father's friend, Stefan Norvitch lives there," explained Katrinka. "Our father wishes us to go to him."

"You do not tell me that you have a father and that he has permitted you to set out alone on such a journey!" exclaimed Sister Elizabeth, looking sharply at Katrinka. "You are sure that you are not running away?"

Katrinka's face crimsoned. "Oh, yes, Matuska," she said, using the pet name, meaning "little mother," "our father wrote us to take the tin box from the cupboard and to go at once to St. Petersburg to Stefan Norvitch. I gave the letter to the priest and then an officer, who said he had been sent by a Grand Duke, came to our house driving a beautiful troika [15] and carried away the box."

"What was in the box, child?" asked the market woman, her smile vanishing.

"I do not know. Father said that Stefan Norvitch should do what he chose with it. He wished Peter to go to the university."

The woman near the stove frowned, but the market woman placed an arm around Katrinka and drew her towards the table.

"When you have eaten you shall tell us more," she said kindly.

She put two large lumps of sugar into a cup, took a little Majolica teapot from the top of the samovar, poured some syrupy tea upon the sugar and then filled the cup with hot water from the samovar.

She set the cup in front of Katrinka and filled another for Peter. Then she served each little one with a small, raw herring with vinegar poured over it. Afterwards she brought honey to the table, cutting a large piece of the comb for each of the children.

The woman who had baked the bread broke the loaf, which was very hot, spread it with butter and laid some of the steaming pieces on plates before them. Then the cheese that Katrinka had bought was produced and cut into slices. Katrinka breathed a great sigh of contentment and looked at Peter, who had been placed on a stool made high enough by the addition of a block of wood and a cushion stuffed with feathers.

The little boy sat with his head hanging down, his hands folded listlessly in his lap. He seemed to have lost interest in the things about him. Katrinka leaned over and held a spoonful of tea to his lips, but he shook his head. His cheeks were red and his eyes dark and heavy-lidded.

"The child is ill," said the market woman, lifting Peter from the stool into her lap. "How long has it been since he has eaten?"

"He had a chicken leg for his dinner about noon."

"That could do him no harm," cried Sister Elizabeth. "Perhaps he is only tired."

"His skin is very hot. He has a fever. What else has he eaten, child?" demanded the market woman.

"Only mushrooms and a few green berries."

"Ah!" exclaimed the market woman. "Do you know good mushrooms from bad ones?"

"Oh, yes, mother taught me."

"But the green berries—how many of those did he eat?"

"Only a few, there were not many."

Sister Elizabeth brushed back Peter's stiff, black hair, then laid her palm against his forehead.

"Eat, my child," she said to Katrinka. "I will look after your brother."

She took Peter from her sister and carried him to the stove, where she undressed him and wrapped him in a warm blanket. Then she made a bed on the shelf in front of the oven. Still holding him in her arms, she offered him hot milk, but he shook his head, pushing the cup away. So she laid him on the shelf and prepared for him a fragrant, hot drink from herbs brought from her storeroom. He took several teaspoonfuls of this, then began to cry softly, whispering that he wanted his mother. But after a while he went to sleep, and the woman with the deep voice joined Katrinka and the market woman at the table.

"Now, my child," said the market woman, when Katrinka, her hunger satisfied for the first time in many days, laid down her knife and fork, "tell us your story."

Katrinka looked thoughtfully at the two friendly faces turned towards her. Then, speaking gently in order not to disturb Peter's sleep, she told the story of the disappearance of her father and mother and of the stranger who had stopped at the church on Easter morning. While she talked the women nodded their heads wisely, and when she had finished the market woman spoke.

"You were lucky, little one, that the men who carried away your father and mother did not burn your house to the ground with you and Peter in it."

The woman seemed to have forgotten that little Peter slept. Her voice rang out. Her sister raised a warning finger. But the market woman went on.

"Things have come to a pretty pass when a peaceful peasant and his wife are torn from their children, because a printing press is found in their possession."

She brought her hand down upon the table with so much force that the dishes rattled. Katrinka glanced at the door. She half expected to see it open to let in a band of Cossacks, or the dark officer who had carried away the tin box. She drew her feet up under her skirts, her eyes wandering from the door to the window, which was much larger than the windows in the izbas at home.

"You are frightening the child," exclaimed Sister Elizabeth, who then rose, and crossing the big, clean kitchen, laid her hand on Peter's head so gently that she did not disturb him.

Presently she returned to where Katrinka and the market woman were sitting. "The little boy is better. His skin is moist. We will all go to bed now and forget our troubles."

They prepared a bed for Katrinka on the shelf beneath the window, and then taking a candle, went into the other room, leaving the door open. Katrinka saw that instead of a shelf they had a bed that stood on four legs. It looked very strange.   She had heard of beds of this kind before, but this was the first one she had ever seen.

CHAPTER XII

"HAVE you ever been to school?" Sister Elizabeth asked Katrinka the following morning after breakfast.

"No, there was no school in our village. Father had the children come to our house after the harvest, to learn to read. But the village policeman came one day and said he had received orders to close the classes, so the children could come no more. They had not yet learned to read."

The woman shook her head. "That was a great pity. But, child, if you would like to, you shall go with me to a real school this morning. It has sixty pupils. In our village every child ten years old knows how to read."

Katrinka glanced at Peter, who sat in the market woman's lap, resting his head against her broad breast, while he sipped hot milk from a cup.

Sister Elizabeth caught the glance. "Peter

is better, but he is not yet well enough to continue the journey to St. Petersburg. Remain here with us for a day or two. You have many miles to travel and you have not been properly nourished for a long time."

Katrinka breathed a sigh of relief. Her back ached and her feet were sore. She was glad indeed to rest in the house of these kind women.

"The school is but two doors away," said the market woman, rising from the table and carrying Peter to a chair by the window. "I pass it on my way to market, and if you would like to visit it, I will take you with me and leave you there in charge of the master."

Katrinka was torn between a desire to see a real school and the feeling that she ought to remain with Peter. The women saw the troubled expression on her face.

"Do not worry about your brother," said Sister Elizabeth. "I am at home all day long, making cakes and bread for my sister to sell at the bazaar. I will take care of him. He is weak and will be content to lie in the big chair until noon, I am sure. He will sleep and will not miss you."

"You are so good," cried Katrinka happily. Her heart felt light and she longed to dance over the smooth kitchen floor, but her feet were sore and she was still a little shy in the presence of the two large women, who seemed so different from the village women she had known.

She took a clean kerchief from her bundle, tied it on her head, smoothed down the plaits of her full skirt and slipped on her dark sandals. Then with a smile at Peter, who smiled back wanly, making no objection to her preparations for leaving him, she joined the market woman,, who, with a basket on her arm, stood ready to go.

It was only a few steps to the school, a low, white-washed building with a green roof and white walls, edged with what looked to Katrinka like wooden lace. When Katrinka and the market woman reached it the children were already gathered in the school yard. Some of the girls wore leather shoes and woolen stockings, while others wore sandals of braided bark with wooden soles, like Katrinka's own. Nearly all of the boys and a few of the girls were barefooted.

Katrinka pulled shyly back as she saw the groups of strange children, but the market woman urged her to make haste as the pupils would be called in presently. Even as she spoke a man with a small beard, and a black coat buttoned over a crossed kerchief, came to the door and rang a bell. All of the children stopped playing and ran towards the school. Immediately Katrinka and the market woman found themselves in a crush of boys and girls.

A moment later Katrinka looked around at the inside of the first real schoolhouse she had ever seen. The market woman and the schoolmaster exchanged a few words and then the master assigned Katrinka to a bench at the back of the room. The market woman nodded to her cheerily, shook hands with the master and disappeared.

The school began with the prayers which the master read. Then there was singing in which Katrinka joined, and after that the classes were called upon to recite, one after another. Each class stood in a little circle around the master.

It was in the middle of the morning that Katrinka felt a shiver run over her, and turn-

ing her eyes from the master, who was busy
with the history class, looked towards the door,
started up, then shrank back, cowering, into
her seat.   Her heart seemed suddenly to jump
into her throat.   In the doorway, his hard,
black eyes fixed on the back of the schoolmaster, was an officer in a blue uniform.   He
stood motionless, his arms folded, listening.

The history lesson went on, and if the master
knew of his strange visitor, he made no sign.
Presently, one of the children asked a question.

"Who takes care of a country that hasn't
any Czar?"

Before the question could be answered, the
officer entered the room, and striding to the
side of the schoolmaster, grasped his shoulder
roughly.   The master looked up, making an
effort to jerk his shoulder from the stranger's
clutch.   As he did so the officer struck him on
the cheek as if he had been a child.   Then he
snatched the book from which the master was
teaching the children, ran over its pages with
his thumb, thrust it into his pocket and announced in a loud voice that the master was
under arrest for teaching treason to Russian
children.

Thrusting the master before him, he then marched him from the room. Immediately two other officers entered the schoolroom, dismissed the pupils, gathered up all of the books they could find, and went out, locking the door behind them.

Katrinka, relieved that the dark man had gone without noticing her, joined the children in the yard. Some of them danced about, glad that school had been closed, but others stood about in groups with serious faces, talking in low voices of what had happened to their master. None of them seemed to know why the school had been closed, but one of the older girls thought it was because mention had been made of the French Revolution during the reading lesson.

Katrinka remained with the children for a little while, listening to their talk, then looking fearfully behind her at every step, hurried back to the market woman's house where she had left Peter. She found Sister Elizabeth stirring up a yellow batter in a big, wooden bowl. To beat the batter she used twigs of white birch instead of a spoon. They were tied together to form a stiff brush. At the sight of Katrinka's white face she paused in her work.

"What is the matter, little one?" she asked. "What brings you back so soon?"

"The school is closed."

"I thought it still had a month to run."

"The police have closed it."

As Katrinka spoke the woman dropped the birch brush, handle and all, into the batter and whirled around. The blood flushed her cheeks, her eyes flashed angrily.

"The police are going too far. It is time somebody reported them to the Czar."

"Why don't you write him a letter?" asked Katrinka.

"What good would that do? My letter would never reach him. It would fall into the hands of some of his officers. He would never see it." She opened the oven door. A great whiff of warm spice-scented air reached Katrinka. Little Peter, who had been put to bed in the sitting room and who had been awakened by the sound of voices, sprang into the room.

"Give me a spice cake, Matuska," he cried.

"When they are done, my child," replied the woman, taking him in her arms and tossing him in the air. The flame of passion that had stained her cheeks had faded. Her voice was calm. She set Peter down and turned to Katrinka. "Come," she said, "we will get a basket ready for the market."

Five minutes later, her basket filled with spice cakes, she bade the children good-by and strode down the brick walk and through the gate to the street.

Katrinka stood under the little stucco portico that shaded the doorway and watched her until she had disappeared. Then she went inside and curled up on the window seat beside Peter.

The house seemed strangely silent, now that the deep voiced woman had gone, and in spite of the sunshine, the warm air laden with spicy fragrance, and the presence of Peter, Katrinka felt lonely. She thought of Marie, busy with the preparations for the wedding feast. There would be three days of dancing on the grass in front of the house. She sighed. Then she recalled the sparkling face of the Grand Duchess Tatiana Nicholovna, who had not been afraid, even of the black browed officer. Some day she would see Tatiana again. She felt sure of it. She snuggled Peter against her side, nestling her cheek against his rough black hair.

"When I have told Tatiana how much we miss our father and mother she will surely ask the Czar to bring them back to us," she murmured softly, her heart comforted at the recollection of the little Grand Duchess.

CHAPTER XIII

TWO days later Katrinka and Peter again set out on their journey. But this time they did not go on foot with only the back and leg of a chicken to guard against starvation.

They rattled away in a tarantas [16] driven by a man who promised the market woman not only to take the children with him to Tsarskoe Seloe but to find for them a night's lodging with a tailor whose address she had given to Katrinka. A package of good things to eat on the journey had also been provided and now, as the carriage set out, the market woman and her sister stood in the portico, their hands on their ample hips, their faces beaming with smiles.

Katrinka and Peter sat on the back seat of the vehicle, their little bundle of clothing under their feet. The driver, a lank man with a shaggy beard, was perched on the front seat. He wore a great wadded coat of blue cloth that looked like a dressing gown. This was confined at the waist by a gay, red girdle. As there was no cushion on the front seat of the tarantas a fat pillow had been stitched to the back of his coat, which was no doubt very comfortable to sit upon but which looked funny when he was bobbing about, getting things ready for the start. He wore on his head a furry-looking stovepipe hat pulled down over his thick, tow-colored hair. From beneath it his eyes peered out good naturedly, so that in spite of the loud voice in which he spoke, the children were not afraid.

When everything was ready for the start he twisted the long reins about his wrists, flourished the ends of them in the air and gave a great shout. Instantly the horses bounded forward, the middle horse trotting, the outside horses galloping, with their heads turned back, their crimson nostrils dilating, their beautiful, great eyes watching the driver's wildly waving arms.

The carriage started with such a jerk that little Peter slipped from his seat, and Katrinka would have followed had she not grasped the side of its slippery cushion and held on with

all her might.   Peter laughed and shouted as
he clambered back into his seat, while the
tarantas rattled down the road, passing the
schoolhouse, which had been turned into a tea
shop, dashing by the bazaar and the old fashioned country inn, and at last gaining the high
road.

The moment the village had been left behind
the horses slackened their pace, and the attitude
of the driver relaxed.   Katrinka, at last feeling secure enough to let go of the seat, turned
and looked back towards the cottage where she
had seen her two kind new friends standing under the portico.   It was already out of
sight.   She waved her hand in its direction,
her eyes misting with tears.   Then, feeling
suddenly afraid and lonely, she slipped her
arm around Peter, gathering him to her.   But
her heart grew lighter as on they went.   The
country fascinated her.   On each side of the
road she saw what seemed to be miles of sunflowers, half grown.   Katrinka felt sure that
when their seeds were harvested they would
provide oil enough for all of Russia to use on
black bread when butter was scarce, or forbidden, as on fast days.

Presently they left the sunflowers behind and came upon fields of rye and buckwheat, and every now and then a little group of log cabins enclosed by high fences made of branches.

The tarantas was an old one. It creaked and rattled, threatening to break into pieces at every rough spot on the road. But to Katrinka it seemed very elegant and she sat up stiffly in self-conscious pride, smiling and nodding with the air of a great lady at the wayside children. Sometimes, when it gave a lurch, she would be almost thrown from the seat, for there were no springs, the braided, willow body being hung between two strong, wooden shafts. The shafts were held together in front by the gayly-painted arch that rose above the middle horse, and in the top of the arch swung a brass bell which clanged constantly. By and by the lurching of the carriage made Katrinka's back and shoulders ache, and in spite of her interest in the strange scenes through which she was passing, she joined Peter, who had again slipped from the seat and was curled upon the floor of the tarantas.

For hours they joggled over the road, stopping at noon to eat the ample lunch which had been prepared for them, while the horses rested and browsed on the roadside grass. As the afternoon wore away, Katrinka's eyes grew heavy and at last her lids dropped. With her arms around Peter, unconscious of the jolting and joggling of the tarantas, she slept soundly, her head resting on her bundle of clothing. She was at last awakened by a terrific lurching of the carriage and the shouts of the driver. Rubbing her eyes, she sat up and looked around. Then she blinked dazedly. The green fields and country roads had disappeared. There stretched before them now a long ribbon of paved street, flanked with lovely villas set in gardens. For a moment Katrinka fancied that she had died and gone to Heaven, everything about her seemed so wonderfully beautiful. Then she saw that she was still in the tarantas and that little Peter was sleeping against her shoulder.

She shook him, calling out to him to sit up and look around. In the street, carriages were dashing up and down. In them were men with handsome uniforms and women with sparkling faces.

On the sidewalks were throngs of children,

and babies in glistening perambulators pushed
by nurses in full skirts, white caps and aprons.
Little boys dashed in and out between the carriages. Many of them were dressed in what
seemed to Katrinka very beautiful uniforms,
and nearly all of them wore shoes and long,
black stockings.

Thrilled with what she saw, she climbed to
the seat, dragging Peter up beside her. She
thought it must be some great fête day that had
brought the people out in such festival attire.
She noticed that the women who drove by in
the carriages wore strange head-dresses, and
she regretted that she had not brought with
her the velvet turban which had belonged to her
mother. Then suddenly she forgot the crowds,
the carriages, the head-dresses. She leaned
forward, her eyes fixed on a little girl who
came galloping down the street towards her
on a white pony—a little girl with sparkling
eyes and wind-blown curls, wearing a black
velvet Tam o' Shanter. And beside her—
Katrinka gasped for breath in her excitement
—beside her, rode a man whose face she knew
as well as she knew the face of her own father,
for his picture hung beside the sacred images

on the wall in her home in the village of Vachok.

The dark beard, the large, kind eyes, the nose—she recognized them at once. They belonged to Nicholas II, the Great White Czar of all the Russias. As the Czar and his daughter approached, Katrinka rose to her feet, making the sign of the cross. The Grand Duchess Tatiana recognized her at once, flashed a merry glance at her and raised her little whip in a gay salute. But the man did not seem to see her; he galloped on, his gaze straight in front. Katrinka strained her eyes after them, then, as the crowd cut off her view, sank back into the seat, her face white with excitement, her heart beating like a drum in her ears.

A moment later the tarantas turned into a side street. The scenes of gayety and splendor were left behind. Instead of gay carriages and people in festival dress, there were throngs of men and women on foot. The pavement was rough and uneven, and the narrow street was bordered with low shops, crowded between weather-beaten dwelling houses. Peddlers and market men shouted their wares. Farmers' wagons and push-carts were everywhere, and among them barefooted boys and girls darted in and out as if bound for destruction. Through this motley assemblage the driver made his way, swinging his whip in a great circle about his head and shouting to the people to make room. After many stops, caused by blockades in the street, the tarantas came out upon a roughly cobbled but comparatively quiet thoroughfare, lined with two-story, brick and stucco houses, the lower parts of which seemed to be used for shops, the second story for dwelling purposes.

Before one of them the carriage drew up with as much of a flourish as the driver could manage.

Katrinka slipped her arm around Peter, wondering what was the matter, while the driver leaped to the ground and went inside a shop. Before it hung a sign on which there was the picture of a huge pair of scissors and a pair of trousers. A flapping board above the door of the neighboring shop displayed a green fish swimming in pale, blue water, and under this there was another board upon which a big key was painted.

While Katrinka was studying the signs, and Peter, who was awake now, was looking wonderingly up and down the street, the driver returned, followed by a little man with a huge nose on which rested a pair of spectacles. The man approached the carriage, nodded at Katrinka and held out his hand.

"I understand from this good man that the widow Baruchi desires that I provide food and shelter for you two little people to-night. My good housekeeper has gone for a little promenade, but I will do the best I can for you until she returns. Hearing that the Czar and the Grand Duchess Tatiana were to ride down the avenue, she must put on her hat and hurry away with the wife of my neighbor, the locksmith."

He smiled, and for a moment Katrinka feared that his face would break into two parts, for the corners of his mouth stretched almost to his ears.

"Come, my good little ones, jump out, and my daughter Catherine will make a cup of tea for you."

He lifted Peter over the wheel and then held out his arms to help Katrinka, whose muscles were stiff from the long ride in the uncomfortable tarantas. Afterwards he turned to the driver.

"Come in with us, my good man, and have some tea and biscuits."

The driver shook his head. "Thank you," he replied, "I have important business to attend to before night." He clambered up into his seat and waved his whip above his head. His horses sprang forward and the tarantas rattled away. The little man smiled one of his alarming smiles and gave a hand to each of the children.

He had left the door of his shop open and as Katrinka crossed the threshold she understood what the huge pair of shears painted on the signboard meant. The little man was a tailor. Inside his shop two young boys sat cross-legged on a table. They were busy finishing coats. They looked up as the children entered, and Katrinka, catching their eyes, smiled and curtesied. The boys smiled sheepishly in return.

The tailor led the children through the shop to a narrow stairway, lighted by what was apparently an open door at the top. As the stairway was not wide enough for them to walk up three abreast, he released their hands and ran nimbly up the stairs ahead of them, pausing at the top and looking down at them with his broad smile. As the children reached the landing, he threw open a door at his right and, with a wave of his hand, motioned them to precede him into the room thus disclosed.

The children crossed the threshold and advanced a couple of steps. Then Katrinka stopped and looked about, her hands clasped on her bosom. Never before had she seen a room like this. There was a white iron bedstead in it, trimmed with golden balls. Instead of benches there were chairs mounted on pieces of wood, curved like sickle blades. On the wall were several sacred pictures surrounded by shining, golden points, and a picture of the Czar in his coronation robes, framed in gold. But the most astonishing thing in the room was a machine in front of the window, at which a young girl sat, working her feet up and down, while she pushed a piece of cloth under what looked like a prancing toy horse. As the children entered the room, she sprang up and stood shyly looking at them.

"The good widow Baruchi has asked us to

give these children shelter for a day or two and to put them on the train for St. Petersburg on Monday or Tuesday morning. You have not yet told me your names, my little ones," he continued, turning to the children after explaining their presence to the young girl.

"My name is Katrinka Petrovski, and this is Peter, my little brother. We are going to St. Petersburg to find our father's friend, Stefan Norvitch."

The young girl who had been sitting at the machine said that her name was Catherine. She had a pretty way of speaking, and although her smile was broad like her father's, it did not alarm Katrinka because her lips were full and red and she had such pretty teeth.

"I will put away your bundle," she said, taking the things tied up in the sheet which Katrinka carried on her arm, "and then we will have tea."

She laid the bundle on the bed and went into another room where she lighted the samovar. While she waited for the water to boil she sat down again at the machine and Katrinka, standing beside her, discovered that when she worked her feet a needle flashed up and down through the cloth, sewing a seam with stitches finer than any Katrinka had ever seen.

The beauty of it was that the stitches taken were all even and that they followed one another with the swiftness of lightning. When Catherine had reached the end of the seam she looked at Katrinka with her broad smile.

"What is it, please?" asked Katrinka, looking at the machine.

"My new dress," replied Catherine, getting ready to start another seam.

"I mean this—the machine—that makes the seam as quickly as one can think."

"Oh!" exclaimed Catherine. "This is a sewing machine. Father has let me take it for a few hours, so that I may finish my dress for Monday. The boys will carry it downstairs again in a few minutes. That is why I have no time to talk until I have finished my seams."

Katrinka, watching Catherine work, thought of Marie Drovski spending days over the seams of her wedding clothes.

"I wish there was a sewing machine in the village of Vachok," she said at last. "The women would have more time to work in the fields and to care for their houses, then."

Catherine did not seem to hear. Katrinka sighed gently and, drawing Peter against her, stood watching the needle flash through the cloth. By and by she spoke again. "Must one be very rich before one can buy a machine like yours?"

Catherine laughed.

"One must have saved at least forty roubles," she said.

"Then," said Katrinka, wisely, "if all the women in the village of Vachok saved a rouble apiece, they could buy a machine and put it in the village hall where all could use it. When I go home again I will tell them about it and how well and quickly it makes a dress. Surely in a day it does as much work as one could do in a week with a needle and thread, Catherine."

Catherine nodded in reply, but she did not stop pushing the cloth under the needle.

CHAPTER XIV

THE PROMENADE OF GIRLS

ON Sunday Katrinka and Peter went to church with the little tailor and his daughter, and at noon on the following day, Catherine finished the dress she was making.

"I was so afraid that I should not have it done for the promenade to-day," she said, holding it up before Katrinka's admiring eyes. "You see, to-day all of the soldiers and sharpshooters, as well as the merchants' sons will be in the park, and every girl in Tsarskoe Seloe will have a new gown for the parade."

Katrinka puckered her brows. In her village everybody wore their new frocks on Easter. Catherine noticed her puzzled expression.

"Do they have no promenade in your village?" she asked, folding the dress over her bosom.

"On Easter Sunday we wear our prettiest

clothes," Katrinka explained. "It is lucky to wear something new on Easter day."

Catherine nodded. "Yes," she said with a coquettish glance at a small mirror that hung above a chest of drawers in the sitting room, "we, too, wear something new on Easter, but for the promenade, on the day after Pentecost, we try to look our best. Do you think I shall look well enough in this to attract the eyes of some good-looking young merchant? I do not wish to marry a soldier."

Katrinka gazed at her new friend, a mystified expression on her face. "I do not understand," she said.

Catherine laughed and began setting the table for dinner. "It is like this. On the Monday after Pentecost all of the girls and young men in Tsarskoe Seloe and the neighboring towns go to the park to promenade. The matchmakers will be there also. The girls wear their best dresses and all of the ornaments they have. If any one of the young men sees and admires one of us, he speaks to a matchmaker and a wedding is arranged. Last year eight of my friends were betrothed on the Monday following Pentecost. I was too young, and father would not let me promenade. We sat on a seat and looked on from one of the terraces."

Katrinka's eyes sparkled. It seemed to her that this was a much better plan than the one pursued in her village, as it gave the girls and young men a chance to see each other before the engagement was announced, and besides, one could choose between several youths, instead of taking the only one offered. By the time dinner was finished and Catherine was dressed and ready to start for the promenade, Katrinka was almost as excited as her friend. Even Peter seemed to realize that something unusual was going to happen, and his little face beamed with eagerness as, clinging to the hand of the tailor, he skipped down the stairs in the wake of the two girls.

To-day all of the shops along the street, which had been so busy the day Katrinka arrived, were closed in honor of the parade of girls. As Catherine and Katrinka turned the corner into the broad avenue leading to the Imperial park where the promenade was to take place, they found themselves in the midst of a merry throng of people, all of whom were hurrying in the same direction. It was a wonderful sight to Katrinka. Her cheeks burned with excitement and her feet in their bark sandals seemed hardly to touch the ground as she danced along the ground beside Catherine.

As they neared the park they could hear the bands mingled with the sound of talk and laughter. Then, presently, the wind brought them whiffs of fragrance and Catherine clapped her hands.

"The lilac hedge is in bloom," she cried. Almost as she spoke Katrinka saw the wonderful hedge of lilacs that surrounds the palace and, in the distance, gleaming above the hedge, the spires of the Imperial Cathedral, tipped with golden balls that looked like huge soap bubbles floating in the air. The noise of merrymaking grew louder. They entered the gates of the park, then paused to gaze at the scene before them.

In the middle of the park there is a little lake, and on its surface canoes and gondolas, flat-bottomed fishing craft and panting motor boats darted about, filled with young men in uniforms. Around the lake marched the girls, all wearing light colors, their feet in slippers, their necks loaded with colored beads. One girl had several silver spoons and forks suspended from a neck ribbon; a part of her wedding dowry, Catherine explained to Katrinka.

As the tailor and his charges approached the lake, a group of young soldiers from the garrison spied them.

"Ah, here comes a pretty girl," cried one, his eyes on Catherine, who tossed her head and began talking rapidly to Katrinka as if she had not heard the remark of the young man.

"She has a good-natured face," replied his companion. "Let us watch her for a while."

"We will cross the bridge," said Catherine. "At the other end of it there are some young merchants. I can tell them by their plain clothes. I do not wish to marry a soldier."

They crossed the bridge and sat down in a kiosk [17] that commanded a view of the lake. Youthful guardsmen strolled by, munching sunflower seeds. Hussars [18] in scarlet jackets walked leisurely up and down. Young merchants in staid-looking business suits leaned against the railings of the bridge, their eyes lingering first on one group of girls and then on another. Middle-aged women flew hither and thither, introducing young people to each other. Katrinka noticed how Catherine's cheeks flushed whenever one of these good-natured-looking matrons drew near.

But, so far, none of the women seemed to have noticed the tailor's daughter, although Katrinka thought her much prettier and more modest-looking than many of the girls who were singled out.

Finally, after they had been sitting in the kiosk for some time, Catherine jumped up and darted away, crying, "Oh, there are some girls whom I know. I will be back presently."

Katrinka's eyes followed Catherine's slim figure in its dress of pale blue muslin, the waist girdled with a bright pink ribbon, until it was lost in the crowd.

"She is much sweeter looking than the others," she sighed. "I hope that some very nice young man proposes for her hand."

Just then the bands struck up a gay air and a young soldier sprang into a clear space near the lake and began to dance. The full skirt of his tunic flew out until it looked like a shelf running around his middle, as he whirled round and round, leaped into the air, or squatted on his heels, waving his arms and taking strange steps in time with the music.

When he had finished his dance, a group of hussars in scarlet jackets laced with gold, jumped into the ring and danced vehemently. They were followed by other soldiers in white cloth jackets buttoned closely about them, who took the steps of their national dances with fiery spirit. As Katrinka watched them her feet began to tap the ground. Oh, if she could only dance with the soldiers! It was the one way she knew of expressing her joy.

Presently a group of soldiers began to sing and the tailor, seeing that Catherine had joined in the parade, suggested that Katrinka and Peter go with him to the children's playground. Katrinka rose reluctantly. She longed to remain in the little kiosk where she could hear the singing and the bands, and watch the dancing. As they crossed the terraces she paused to look back at the gay scene set in the midst of the exquisite park.

She could not understand how the tailor could willingly turn his back upon such a picture.

But presently she was thrilled anew. They

had entered another park, in the center of which had been set up a tall ship's mast, surrounded near its foot by a wide piece of rope netting, very strong and close-meshed. Dozens of boys and girls were climbing into the rigging of the mast and jumping into the net where they bounced up and down on its yielding surface. Peter clapped his hands and pulled the tailor in the direction of the net.

"I want to climb up the pole and jump," he cried.

"That is why I brought you here, my good boy. And you, Katrinka, would you like to try your skill at climbing the mast?"

"Oh, yes," cried Katrinka, forgetting the dancing soldiers in her eagerness to take part in this strange game. "Come, Peter."

With Peter's hand in hers she ran over the greensward toward the mast, and presently was at its very top. For a moment she poised in the rigging, then flew through the air, landing in the elastic net.

All of the other children were dressed in gay colors, their feet encased in well-fitting boots or slippers, and yet, in spite of her dull dress, her large, ill-fitting sandals, it was presently upon Katrinka that all eyes were centered, as again and again she climbed the mast, paused for a moment in the rigging, and then with arms extended, came flying down through the air like a swift, brown-plumaged, little bird, until at last, quite breathless, she leaped from the net and joined a group of boys and girls who stood looking on.

A band from the larger park appeared and began playing a series of national airs. The children formed a ring around it, many of them singing the words of the familiar tunes in shrill, piping voices.

By and by several of the girls and boys detached themselves from the surrounding circle and began to dance. From a distance they looked like butterflies in their pretty, light-colored clothing. Katrinka watched them, her eyes sparkling, her small hands clasped. Then, forgetting her peasant's dress, her awkward shoes, she sprang into their midst. It seemed to her that she was made of steel springs as she leaped and whirled as the hussar had done, her feet in their clumsy sandals keeping perfect time with the music.

The thought flashed through her mind that

all of her life, as she had danced down the village street to her own singing, she had been preparing for this moment, when she could express in rhythm with this wonderful music all the delight that she felt in the sunlight, the flowers, the very joy of living. As she danced, her face flushed, her eyes flashed, the dimples came and went in her cheeks and, as when she had sprung from the mast, all eyes were centered on her.

At last the music ended with a crash. There was the sound of hand-clapping and shouted huzzas. Suddenly shy, Katrinka joined the circle of spectators. Then, noticing for the first time the many eyes that were fixed upon her, she blushed furiously and looked around for the little tailor. He was crossing the empty space in front of the band, leading Peter by the hand. She ran to him and hid her flaming face against his sleeve. She was suddenly self-conscious. She fancied that the people were looking at her because of her coarse, homespun skirt and her awkward sandals.

The tailor laid his hand on her shoulder. "My good child," he began, then paused. They had reached the edge of the crowd. Katrinka

raised her eyes questioningly, but quickly lowered them again.   Directly in front of her
stood a tall, fine-looking officer, his coat covered with glittering medals.

CHAPTER XV

KATRINKA DANCES FOR THE CZAR

THE officer held his hat in his hand and in it there was a handful of silver coins.

"His Imperial Highness requests the child to dance again," he said, smiling at Katrinka. She shook her head, her frightened face hidden in the tailor's sleeve.

"Come, come, my good little one," said the tailor, "look up. Did you not understand?"

Katrinka looked up and curtesied shyly.

"His Imperial Highness requests the child to dance for him again," repeated the officer, still holding out his hat containing the silver coins.

Katrinka's lip quivered. She looked at the tailor beseechingly, and seeing that his eyes were fixed on the terrace above the park, followed them with her own. Then, forgetting her fright, she stood staring in speechless amazement.

Under a gayly striped awning was gathered

a little group of men and women.   The women were dressed in trailing, white gowns, their heads shaded by lace-covered parasols.   With them were several officers and four little girls. Among the latter Katrinka recognized the Grand Duchess Tatiana.   Then her eyes swept the faces of the officers.   In their midst she saw the Czar, dressed in a dark-green uniform girdled with crimson.   Beside him stood a boy, a little taller than Peter, wearing a white blouse and knickerbockers.

Katrinka forgot her shyness.   "Oh," she cried, "it is the Czar, the Little Father."   She started towards the terrace.   "I wish to speak to him—to ask him to send back our father and mother from Siberia."

"Ssh!" warned the tailor, gripping Katrinka's shoulder.   "What are you talking about, my good child?"

Something in the tailor's voice stopped Katrinka.   She looked up at the officer.   There was a scowl on his forehead.

"What is it the child asks?" he demanded.

"I wish to speak to the Czar," cried Katrinka.

"That is impossible!"   The man waved his

hand in the direction of the musicians. The music began. "Here is some silver for the child," he continued, pouring the money into the tailor's outstretched hands. "His Imperial Highness requests her to dance again."

"And may I speak to him, please, afterwards?" asked Katrinka, beseechingly.

"If you have a message for His Imperial Highness, give it to me. It is impossible for you to speak to His Majesty."

Katrinka sighed. "Will you say to him, please, that my father, Peter Petrovski, and my mother, Marie Petrovski, are in Siberia and that Peter and I are very lonely without them, and sometimes hungry. Will you ask him to return them to us?"

The officer frowned. "You are wasting time," he said. "Their Imperial Highnesses wish to see you dance. The music has already begun."

He turned upon his heel, and the next moment, sure that her message would be delivered, Katrinka sprang lightly into the space in front of the musicians. Once again her feet beat gay time to the martial strains. Then, suddenly, her head drooped, her hands hung listtessly at her sides, her movements became gentle as an evening wind, melting as a sigh. As if understanding her change of mood, the music softened, grew slow and wonderfully sweet. The child's dancing was like a prayer. Tears rose to the eyes of the onlookers. Katrinka was telling them a story. They realized it, but could not understand. Gradually the music died away and slowly Katrinka sank to her knees, her arms stretched out towards the terrace on which the Czar stood watching her. A moment later, she bounded to her feet again, waving her hands and skimming the ground in eager joy. She kicked off her bark sandals; the bandages, loosened by her rapid movements, slipped to the ground. Heedless of them, she danced on, her bare, brown feet twinkling as she whirled and leaped and spun around and around. Suddenly the music stopped with a crash of cymbals. Katrinka sprang into the air with outstretched arms, then sank again to her knees, her eyes on the bearded face of the Czar.

There was the sound of hand-clapping on the terrace, and then the Czar and his little party turned, and without a backward glance, walked away. Katrinka looked after them in disappointed amaze, again self-conscious and awkwardly shy. She ran to the tailor.

"Let us go home, please," she murmured.

The tailor laid his hand gently on her shoulder. "As you wish, little one," said he, kindly.

They elbowed their way through the crowds, which with holiday fickleness, had already forgotten Katrinka and her dancing and were listening to a group of soldiers who had come to the children's park and were singing rollicking airs.

"We will go back and watch the parade," said the tailor, taking Katrinka's hand. "We will see if any of the young merchants has taken a fancy to our Catherine."

"Do you think the officer will give my message to the Czar?" Katrinka asked, looking wistfully up into the tailor's face.

"Nobody can answer that. Many another child has sent messages to the Little Father, but I am afraid their prayers seldom reach him. But keep a brave heart. My pocket is heavy with the silver that the great ladies and gentlemen sent to you. Perhaps after you arrive in

St. Petersburg, Stefan Norvitch will know of some way to reach the good Czar."

In the Imperial park the parade was still going on but Catherine was nowhere in sight. They walked around the lake and crossed the bridge without finding her, and then, just as they were making their way to the kiosk, they caught sight of her, sitting in a grotto with one of the matchmakers and a young merchant.

She looked so happy that Katrinka felt sure she was already betrothed. As they approached, she saw them, and leaving the young man and the matchmaker, came running towards them. Presently the matchmaker shook hands with the young man, who left the kiosk and strolled towards the bridge. The matchmaker beckoned to the tailor who immediately joined her. Then Catherine confided to Katrinka and Peter that, if her father approved, she would be married the following month to the young merchant whom she had just met. Katrinka kissed her gravely: "I hope you will be happy, Catherine," she said, glancing towards the bridge where the young merchant was strolling. The thought occurred to her that if she had been in Catherine's place, she would have chosen the hussar who flew around so fast that his tunic stood out like a shelf, or the young soldier in the full, green trousers and the white jacket, laced with gold, whose feet moved so nimbly in the peasant dances.

CHAPTER XVI

A GREAT many trains run between Tsarskoe Seloe and St. Petersburg, but the little tailor decided that the best one for Katrinka and Peter to take was the one that left Tsarskoe Seloe at about eleven o'clock in the morning and reached St. Petersburg half an hour later.

"For," he said with one of the smiles that seemed to split his face in halves, "if it should turn out that this good man, Stefan Norvitch, whom these little ones are setting out to find, should be away from home, time must be allowed for them to find some shelter before night falls."

Consequently, Katrinka and Peter, escorted by Catherine and her father, set off in the direction of the station almost as soon as breakfast was over. Katrinka was very silent. She had never seen a train of cars before and would

149

have preferred continuing the journey to St. Petersburg on foot, and so she told the tailor before they started out. But he refused to listen to such a suggestion. "Peter is far too small to undertake so long a journey on foot," he said. "The child would be ill before you reached the city. Besides, you would be three days on the road for a certainty, and would have to sleep in strange houses. Supposing you should meet the officer who took your tin box? How could you prevent him from taking the handful of silver that the Imperial family sent you for your pretty dancing? Come, my good child, let us not talk nonsense."

At the mention of the officer who had taken the tin box, Katrinka lost her courage. Very meekly she tied her kerchief over her head and crossed her shawl about her shoulders. As she pulled Peter's cap over his stiff, black hair, she bent and kissed him.

Peter scowled fiercely, then suddenly threw his arms around his sister's neck and returned her salute with fervor.

"Do not be afraid, Katrinka," he said; "Peter will take care of you."

Katrinka was surprised at his remark for

she had said nothing of her fears. She was also pleased. There was something brave and sturdy about her little brother. She felt her confidence returning.

"We are ready," she said, turning to the tailor, who immediately threw open the door. Katrinka started towards it, then paused, and moving close to the tailor, spoke to him shyly as if fearing to offend the kind-hearted little man.

"Peter and I would like to make Catherine a wedding present, but we do not know where to go, nor what to get."

She laid two roubles on the table, the price she had received for the samovar. "Yesterday, when I saw the girl in the parade with the silver spoons and the soup ladle, that were a part of her wedding dowry, around her neck, I wished that I could give a silver ladle to Catherine. But I did not know where to find a shop that sold such things. Will you please buy the ladle for her and add it to her dowry?"

The tailor picked up the coins and handed them back to Katrinka. "Thank you, my good little one. That is too great a gift. Catherine would appreciate far more the string of blue beads that you wear. Leave them and I will gladly add them to her dowry with your blessing."

Katrinka unfastened the string of blue beads that had cost only a few kopecks, kissed them and placed them in the tailor's hand. Then, as Catherine entered the room, dressed in a woolen frock and wearing a red cloth Tam o' Shanter, they set out towards the station which they reached long before train time.

The tailor walked with Katrinka, advising her all the way about what she was to do when she reached St. Petersburg. First of all, she was to ask a porter to show her where she could find a directory giving the addresses of the residents of St. Petersburg. If she was unable to find the name of Stefan Norvitch, she must ask somebody to help her. When she had found the address, she was told to ask what street car would take her to the corner nearest where Stefan Norvitch lived. If, when she arrived at his house, she found that he was not at home, the tailor told her to wait on the door-step or to go to one of the neighbors. Then, if it grew late and still he had not returned,

she must ask a policeman to show her the way
to a number which he had written on a card
and pinned inside her blouse.

"It is the address of my sister," he explained.
"Tell her your story. She has a large house
and will give you a night's lodging and a good
breakfast. If, on the next day you cannot find
Stefan Norvitch, return to Tsarskoe Seloe and
I will see that you are started safely for your
home in the village of Vachok."

Over and over again the tailor repeated his
directions, warning Katrinka that St. Petersburg was a very large city, and telling her that
she must carry her bag of silver pinned securely
in her pocket.

He was repeating this to her for the tenth
time, when the train with its bright blue, tan
and dull-brown cars pulled into the station.
The tailor explained that the blue and tan cars
were the first and second class coaches. He
then put Katrinka and Peter into one of the
dull-brown cars, which were third-class and
very cheap. The car was fitted with long,
wooden benches. These were presently filled
with men and boys and a stout, dark-skinned

woman, who immediately produced a little tea-pot and a tiny lamp and began to brew her-self a glass of tea.

Catherine embraced Katrinka and kissed Peter. The tailor patted their shoulders, warn-ing them again to be careful. There was a shrill whistle, a terrific jolt and the train began to move. Katrinka thrust her head out of the window for one more glimpse of her friends, then sat up very straight, blinking to keep back the tears. She slipped an arm around Peter who looked up at her, and seeing the tears in her eyes, patted her hand and again promised to take care of her. Katrinka smiled in spite of herself. Never before had little Peter been so dear. Perhaps the tailor had told him that he must take care of his sister.

CHAPTER XVII

THE crowd at the St. Petersburg station was so confusing that, for the first few minutes after leaving the train, Katrinka stood looking about her dazedly, forgetting the tailor's careful directions.

Red-capped porters, carrying luggage and shouting at the top of their voices, were rushing back and forth; automobiles and horses dashed in, picked up richly dressed men and women and dashed away again. Bells on horse cars and trolleys clanged and jangled. And nobody paid the least attention to Katrinka and Peter, as they stood, hand in hand, near the door of the station.

Twice Katrinka approached a red-capped boy to ask him to show her where there was a directory, but each time the boy ran away before she could get the big word out of her mouth. After her second attempt a tall woman in a black-and-white suit, with red roses on her hat, smiled at Katrinka, passed her, then turned and came back.

"What do you want, child?" she asked, speaking very slowly and with great exactness. "Can I be of help to you?"

Katrinka explained as quickly as she could that she wished to see a directory where she could learn the street on which her father's friend, Stefan Norvitch, lived. She was hurrying on in her explanations when the woman held up her hand:—"I am a stranger— an American—I cannot understand. You go too fast," she said laughingly. "Now repeat. But speak slowly, oh, very slowly. Where do you wish to go?"

Katrinka began again, but before she had spoken half a dozen words the woman again held up her hand.

"More slowly—a few words at a time. Now, again."

Very deliberately Katrinka started once more, but it was hard to speak slowly when there was excitement and shouting all about her. But at last, after many trials, she managed to make the pretty, laughing woman understand what she wanted, and a few minutes later she and little Peter were seated in a trolley car beside this wonderful, new friend who had such difficulty in understanding Katrinka's simple speech.

As they rumbled down the street, the lady wrote something on a little card and gave it to Katrinka, telling her that it was the address of Stefan Norvitch which she had looked up in the directory before leaving the station. Then she spoke to the conductor, and presently with a smile and a nod, left the children to continue their journey alone.

After a long and interesting ride, during which Peter turned his back to the inside of the car and kneeling on the seat, kept his face plastered to the window for fear of missing some of the wonderful scenes outside, the conductor told Katrinka that she had reached her destination. He stopped the car long enough to point out the way she was to take, telling her to ask a policeman, who stood on the corner, which was the number she wanted to find.

But this was unnecessary, for Katrinka herself discovered Stefan Norvitch's number right away. The house was built of red brick and had four stories. Its window sashes and door-way were painted sky-blue. In front of an open window a small man with a gray mustache sat playing an accordeon.

As the children hesitated at the steps, he looked from the window, nodded, and with the accordeon still in his hands, leaned out and asked what they wanted. Katrinka explained that she was looking for Stefan Norvitch, whereupon he opened the door and directed her to go upstairs.

"Stefan Norvitch is at his business, but you will find his housekeeper at home."

There was a door at the head of the stairs and, hanging beside it, a little iron mallet. Katrinka rapped gently with her knuckles. There was no answer. She rapped again more loudly. She could hear somebody walking about inside. She waited—then with all her might, rapped again. Still the door remained closed. Suddenly the man with the accordeon appeared at the foot of the stairs.

"Use the knocker. The woman is as deaf as a post."

Katrinka, thereupon, took the mallet and hammered upon the door. It was thrown open immediately and Katrinka looked into the living room of Stefan Norvitch, her father's friend.

Until this moment she had thought no room could be more beautiful and luxurious than the sitting-room where she had first seen Catherine at work upon the sewing-machine. But this room, although plain, was even more pleasing. Its walls were light buff and there were shelves running all around them filled with books.   In the middle of the room stood a square, black table, and on it a samovar.   Beside the window there was a leather chair.   It was so large that one could curl up and sleep in it.   Near one of its padded arms was a little stand on which there was a candle and some books. There were also other chairs and a desk littered with papers. A great many pictures were tacked upon the wall, but before Katrinka had a chance to more than glance at them, the little, wrinkled woman who had opened the door, put her ear very close to Katrinka's mouth and asked what the children wanted.   With great difficulty Katrinka explained to the woman why she had come, and soon she and Peter were sitting at the black table, drinking tea from little glasses and nibbling cakes and biscuits.

After they had finished their tea, the woman left them, and when Katrinka pushed open the door leading into the kitchen to ask if she could be of help, she discovered that the woman was no longer there. She had evidently gone down a back stairway to the street. Katrinka then returned to the sitting room and waited for what seemed hours.

Peter grew restless, but finally went to sleep in the big chair by the window. Downstairs the man with the gray mustache played on the accordeon. A clock on the mantel ticked minute after minute away. The loneliness oppressed Katrinka and she was about to go downstairs to sit on the doorstep in front of the house when there were steps in the hall, a key was turned in the lock and the door opened. Katrinka, who had been kneeling in front of the book shelves, sprang to her feet, her little hands clasped together, her eyes wide and frightened.

The door opened slowly to admit the largest man Katrinka had ever seen. His hair and beard were white and bushy, and his eyes burned strangely beneath overhanging, white brows.   Tucked under his arm were two large books with red covers.   He wore a long coat, confined at the waist by a rope.

He looked at Katrinka and then his eyes fixed themselves on Peter who still slept in the big chair.

"Well, well!   What does this mean?" he asked, and it seemed to Katrinka that his voice sounded like the rumbling of distant thunder.

"Are you Stefan Norvitch?" she asked, looking fearfully at Peter who had been awakened by the strange voice and was now sitting up, rubbing his eyes.

The man threw off his coat.   "Yes," he replied, "I am Stefan Norvitch.   And who may you be?"

"I am the daughter of Peter Petrovski, who was taken away in the night."

The great man strode across the room, and taking Katrinka's face between his palms, looked into her eyes.   Then he turned and looked at Peter, brushed his hands across his eyes and nodded his bushy head.

"Welcome, my children," he said, and the walls seemed to echo his words.   He picked up Peter and holding him in one arm sat down in the big chair by the window. In front of the chair there was a low, leather-covered stool. He pointed to it.

"Sit there," he said, speaking to Katrinka, "and tell me why you have come and where Peter Petrovski has gone."

Katrinka sat down on the little stool. But she did not know where to begin her story, Finally Stefan Norvitch helped her.

"You say your father was taken away—who took him and why?"

"He and mother were taken away in the night. We do not know why they were taken, but our neighbor said it was because father had a printing press."

"No doubt," rumbled Stefan Norvitch. "But go on with your story. Have you had no word from your parents since they were taken away?"

"Oh, yes," said Katrinka, and then with her eyes on the window through which she could see the stars as they came out in the sky, she told the story of the messenger who had come to the church on Easter morning, of the officer who had demanded the tin box and of the long days when she and Peter had suffered from loneliness and hunger.

In the meantime the housekeeper was moving about the room, setting the table and preparing supper. Peter delightedly sniffed the odor of the good things to eat that came from the kitchen.

"And the Czar sent you silver when you danced, yesterday?" asked Stefan Norvitch, when at last the story was ended.

"Yes. An officer brought it in his cap."

Stefan Norvitch breathed a great sigh. "He is very fond of children and yet hundreds of them are orphaned all over the country." Very gently he smoothed Katrinka's hair. "I will do what I can for Peter Petrovski's little ones," he said, then paused. "How would you like to have me tell you about your father, when he was a little boy?"

"Like me?" demanded Peter, thrusting his fingers into Stefan Norvitch's gray beard.

"As you will be, pretty soon. When I first saw him he was as tall as Katrinka, a fine, upstanding lad, with stiff black hair and bright eyes. He had come to St. Petersburg with his father, who knew how to read, and who had come to my store to buy a primer for his little son. I liked the boy and asked his father, who had many other children, to leave him with me, to help in the store. I promised to pay a rouble a week for his services."

"Did my father live here with you?" asked Katrinka, eagerly, clasping her hands against her breast.

"Yes, and many a night I have come home to find him curled up in this very chair, sound asleep, as I found Peter a few minutes ago. He was a good boy and worked hard and, by and by, he knew as much about the shop as I did myself. After the first year I gave him more money and would have made him a partner, but his health broke down. The doctors said it would be better for him to work in the fields and so, with regret, I bade him good-by one morning, and I have never seen him since. But I knew that wherever he was he was doing his duty. I am grieved to think that he has been sent away."

Stefan Norvitch dropped his chin into his hand and sat lost in thought. Katrinka looked at him.   When his sharp eyes were hidden, his face was sad.

"I think you are very wise, and very good, Stefan Norvitch," she said at last.   "You will know how to bring father and mother back to us."

"I will do my best, little one," replied Stefan Norvitch.   "But now we will have supper."

He drew a chair up to the table, placed on it the two large, red books that he had brought home, and then swung Peter to the top of them with a bounce.

CHAPTER XVIII

"DO nearly all of the people in the world live in St. Petersburg?" asked Katrinka when, supper over, Stefan Norvitch with Peter in his arms, returned again to the big chair by the window.

"No, child, only a small part of all the people in the world live in St. Petersburg," he replied. "In fact all this great city, all of the roofs you see from the window, the great building over there with the many lights, which has so many rooms that it would take all day and all night just to step into each one and out again and which is called the Winter Palace, have been here but a little more than two hundred years."

"What do you mean, Stefan Norvitch?" asked Katrinka, her eyes wide with wonder. "Hasn't St. Petersburg always been here ever since the world began?"

"I mean that only two hundred and fifty

years ago where this great city stands to-day there was only a marsh covered with long grass and muddy water. The Czars lived in Moscow [19] in those days and Russia had no railroads and no battleships. Then one day about two hundred and forty-five years ago a baby boy was born in the royal palace at Moscow who, when he grew up, changed everything in our country. His name was Peter and he became known throughout the world as Peter the Great."

"Tell us more about him, please," said Katrinka, snuggling her cheek against Stefan Norvitch's knee.

"His mother was an Empress [20] whose days were so filled with other things that she let her little boy grow up without any training whatever. He had no tutors and no hours for study. He spent his days as he saw fit, playing with drums and swords. This would have spoiled some children but it seemed to be good for Peter. Having no one to teach him what he wanted to know he went about finding things out for himself. He asked questions of everybody and whenever he saw strangers on the streets of Moscow he stopped to talk with them, asking them from what country they had come and begging them to tell him something about the habits and customs of their people.

"On one of his walks he saw a boat going against the wind. He could not rest until he had learned to manage such a boat. Then he built one, and although afraid of the water, he sailed in it constantly. But it was too small for a long voyage, so he set about building a larger one. In this he visited other countries, and finding that they had battleships to protect them in time of war he made up his mind to have a navy built. He picked out fifty young noblemen and sent them to foreign countries to learn the business of building ships. Peter himself went to Holland, where he put on workman's clothes and toiled from early morning until night in the shipyards. The people of his own and other courts were horrified. It seemed out of place for a young Emperor to hurry away from a dinner given to him by a king, perhaps, to get into his working clothes, and in grime and dirt, work like a common laborer.

"But Peter was so eager to learn that he did not care what people said. He found out all about shipbuilding, and returning to Russia established a navy. Then he set about learning other trades. Once he came upon a traveling dentist who had set up a chair in the market place and was practicing his craft. Peter watched him for a while, then asked him to come to the palace. He taught Peter the use of the instruments and Peter afterwards insisted upon filling the teeth of many of his friends. Again he met a German lady wearing an enameled watch. He stopped her, asked if he could examine her watch, and having done so, returned it to her. Later he learned the trade of watch-making and had it taught in Russia.

"While he was abroad he looked into one trade after another and engaged men who held high positions in various factories and institutions to return with him to Russia and to teach his people all that they knew.

"He discovered that in the great nations which he visited the people did not fling themselves to the ground when their rulers passed, as they did in Russia. Therefore, when he came back to his own country, he forbade his subjects to kneel with their foreheads in the

dust whenever they saw him. He opened
schools and colleges. In the past, people who
owed money that they could not pay, were
bound to posts and beaten. Peter stopped this
punishment. He also ordered the women in
Russia to uncover their faces. Before his day
they had gone with their features heavily veiled
as the women do in Turkey. He also ordered
the men to shave off their beards. Formerly
the Russian months were different from the
months in other countries—January was called
September, February was October, and so on.
Peter made a new calendar so that Russian
months agreed with those in the rest of Europe,

"Then he started to build St. Petersburg.
It was a terrible task to fill in the marshes and
so make ground on which to put up buildings
and to lay out streets. The nobles belonging
to his court objected to the undertaking. But
Peter was stubborn. He said that Moscow
was too far away from Europe so he started
the new capital and built the great Winter
Palace.

"Peter, himself, did not live in the Winter
Palace. Like all truly great men, he had
simple tastes. He occupied a tiny cottage on

the shore of the river Neva, and he disliked so much having servants to wait on him that he invented a table with an arrangement of ropes and pulleys so that the dishes could be removed and changed from downstairs. The table seated twenty people and was furnished with a bell which was rung as a signal to the servants below that the time had come to work the pulleys and change the plates. Even when every place at the table was occupied, no servants appeared in the dining room and Peter could almost forget their existence."

Stefan Norvitch paused. Little Peter sat up.

"Tell us some more about Peter," he demanded. "Did he have black hair like mine?"

"Yes, and he was very tall and very strong. He could lift a young ox in his arms as easily as you can lift a puppy."

"Was it Peter the Great who freed the serfs?" asked Katrinka.

"No," replied Stefan Norvitch with a sigh. "It was he who first made slaves of them."

"But you said he was good?"

"He was. He thought that he was helping the people when he made serfs, or slaves as they call them in other countries, of free people."

Katrinka's dark brows drew together. She had heard her mother tell how, not so very many years ago, nearly all of the men and women who worked in the fields had been serfs, and how little children were often taken from their parents and sold to far away landowners.

"I do not understand," said Katrinka. "If Peter the Great was good why did he make slaves of the people?"

"He did it to prevent them from wandering here and there like bands of gypsies, as they had done before his day. For a time his plan worked well. But by and by the landowners discovered how easy it was to raise money to spend in the cities by selling some of their serfs to other landowners in need of workers. For example, a noble living on the far borders of the country might need children to care for his sheep. He would send word, therefore, to some noble having on his estate more children than he required, to send two or three of these little ones to him. In return for the children he paid a few roubles. It was no uncommon thing in those days for little boys and girls only five or six years of age to be torn from their parents and sent to work among strangers, growing up unloved and lonely. All over Russia broken-hearted mothers and fathers mourned the loss of their little ones.

"Then at last a great Czar came to the throne. His name was Alexander and he was the grandfather of Nicholas, the present ruler, whom you call the Little Father. He freed the serfs but, alas, the people did not understand him and the good he wanted to do. He was killed with a bomb as he was driving along the frozen river, Neva, in his sleigh."

Stefan Norvitch paused and passed his large hand over his eyes. Katrinka waited for some time for him to go on but he seemed lost in thought. At last she spoke.

"I wish, Stefan Norvitch, that you would tell us a story about the Czar when he was a little boy, before he was Emperor of all the Russias. Then, when you have done, tell us about Tatiana. Her eyes look full of courage and she was not afraid even of the officer who sat beside the driver on the front seat of the carriage and scowled fiercely when she told him to lift Peter and me up beside her and to take us to the bazaar."

Stefan Norvitch laughed.

CHAPTER XIX

"VERY well, little Katrinka; I will tell you all I know about the Emperor Nicholas and his family."

Katrinka sat up, her hands clasped on her breast.

"Will you begin, please, with when he was a little boy?"

"Of course, child, if you wish it, for after all, a man is only a grown-up child.

"When Nicholas was a little boy I used to see him frequently on the streets of St. Petersburg. He usually wore a Cossack's uniform and was accompanied by one or another of his tutors, of whom he had a great many. It seemed to me that he had a sad face and I often wondered if he would live to manhood. His father was very severe with him, making his life as hard as that of any peasant. He had to get up at six in the morning. His lessons began at seven. These were not finished until noon, although he had some time for recreation between nine and ten. After his lessons had been completed, he usually walked for an hour with one of his tutors, dined at two and then rested or played until five, when studies were again taken up and carried on until seven in the evening.

"From seven until eight there were gymnastics and then supper. In the evening, lessons were reviewed, and at ten o'clock the little boy went to bed.

"Once, when he was about sixteen, he came to my shop and bought some books. His manner was simple and there was a merry twinkle in his eyes, which were brown and clear. His voice was pleasing and, although he was small and slight for his years, he had a good figure. I liked him. But it takes more than a kind heart and a pleasing manner to make a good Czar. What a Czar needs is intelligence, honesty and strength of character.

"A few days after Nicholas came to my shop, he went to Germany to attend the wedding of his uncle, Sergius, to a German Princess. The bride had a lovely younger sister named

Alix, a sweet, laughter-loving girl of twelve
This little girl was learning to cook and make
her own dresses for, although she was a princess and her sister was marrying an uncle of
young Nicholas, her father was very poor and
was bringing up his daughters in a sensible
manner.

"Alix and Nicholas, who was then called the
Czarevitch, which means 'son of the Czar,'
were the youngest members of the wedding
party. While preparations for the wedding
were going on they were constantly together,
rowing on the river, playing tennis, dancing
and driving about the little German village of
Darmstadt, where the marriage was to take
place. This little girl had only two marks [21]
a week for spending money, and in those days
she did not dream that a few years later she
would marry the young boy with whom she
played, and so become Empress of all the Russias. But she did.

"In these early days of her life, the Princess
Alix was so full of joy that her sisters and
father gave her the nickname of 'Sunny.' It
is small wonder that the young Czarevitch
Nicholas was charmed with her. Her eyes

were a deep grayish-blue, fringed with curling, black lashes. Her hair was brown and glossy, her features, beautifully regular. She had a little brown mole at the left of her mouth that looked like an old-fashioned beauty patch and served to bring out the fairness of her complexion. She was tall and slender, and walked gracefully.

"She and the young Czarevitch had a delightful week together; then the young man returned to his studies in St. Petersburg, and the little girl resumed her simple life in the German village. Not long after this the health of the Czarevitch broke down and his father, realizing that he had been working too hard, sent him on a trip around the world.

"When, having completed his trip, Nicholas returned to Russia, the question of his marriage was almost immediately brought up. His father had in mind several powerful princesses, any one of whom he believed would make a good wife for Nicholas. But Nicholas had ideas of his own. Back in his head he carried the picture of a little German girl whom he had met in the village of Darmstadt. Her beautiful, sunny face came between him and the powerful princesses whom his father favored. He told his father that if he must marry, he would take for his bride the young Princess Alix of Darmstadt. The Czar was annoyed at this announcement, but the young Czarevitch was stubborn. They argued the matter for days, and at last Nicholas prevailed upon his father to let him go again to Germany to see the young princess.

"Then began a very happy time. The young people spent long days together, falling more and more deeply in love. There seemed to be but one question upon which they could not agree and that was religion. The Princess Alix had been brought up in the English church and was, therefore, an Episcopalian. The Czar was the head of the Greek church. According to the laws of Russia, the throne may never be occupied, or shared, by any one not of the Greek-Catholic faith. In most royal marriages the bride changes her faith as easily as she changes her gown, but the young Princess Alix was devoted to her church. She could not easily be persuaded to give it up.

"Very learned men in the Greek church were sent to the little German village to explain the faith they wished her to adopt. The young princess spent hours with them arguing over points that were not clear, and more than once she asked them questions that they found it difficult to answer. Finally word was sent to Nicholas and his parents that, although Alix still looked upon the teachings of her own church as right and would not declare them wrong, she would consent to join the Greek church. She said that she could pray as well in the Greek church as in her own.

"About this time, the father of Nicholas, Alexander III, was taken ill. He sent for Princess Alix. She hurried to his bedside, and then followed the formal betrothal between her and Nicholas II, which in Russia is as binding as a marriage. Soon after the betrothal was announced, the Czar died, and three weeks later, while the court was still in mourning, Alix and Nicholas were married. Before the ceremony the young princess changed her name from Alix to Alexandra, which is the name of a saint in the Russian church, for it is a law of the country that nobody can sit upon the throne who is not named after a saint.

"During the next ten years four little girls

were born to Alexandra and Nicholas. They were named Olga, Tatiana, Anastasia and Marie. They were beautiful children, but none of them could occupy the throne in case of the Czar's death. So the Czar and Czarina prayed for a son. For a long time their prayers seemed vain, then just as they were despairing of having a son, another child, a boy, was born.

"At the palace there was great rejoicing and the Czar was so delighted over the new baby that he gave himself up almost entirely to his family, letting his uncles, who are called Grand Dukes, manage the affairs of the country as they saw fit.

"The small boy who, if he grows up, will be the next Czar of Russia, is a handsome child. But few people have seen him. So many attempts have been made to destroy him that his parents do not let him appear in public. The four girls may be met any day, driving and riding about the streets in the village of Tsarskoe Seloe, but one never gets a glimpse of the little Czarevitch, whose name is Alexis Nicholaevitch, which means Alex, son of Nicholas, for 'vitch' at the end of a name al-

ways stands for 'son of.' The names of the
Czar's daughters end in 'ovna,' which means
'daughter of.' "

"Then the Grand Duchess Tatiana's name is
Tatiana Nicholovna, because she is the
daughter of Nicholas," interrupted Katrinka.
"And yet I am called Katrinka Petrovski, and
Peter's name is Peter Petrovski."

"It would be quite right to call you Katrinka
Petrovna, and your brother, Peter Petrovitch,
since your father's first name is Peter."

"Katrinka Petrovna is a lovely name,"
mused Katrinka. "I think that after this you
may call me that."

"Very well," rumbled Stefan Norvitch, smiling. "But do you want to hear more of the
little boy who, if he lives, will some day be the
Czar of Russia?"

"Yes, please," said Katrinka. "Does Tatiana see him every day?"

"He plays with his sisters, and orders them
about as he sees fit. They adore him and spoil
him. But, as I said, attempts have already
been made to take this small boy's life. Once,
when he was only a baby, the palace wells were
poisoned. Later, a bomb was placed under the

dining-room in the Winter Palace. It exploded, fortunately, before the Czar and his family arrived, wrecking the room, but doing no other harm. His father and mother consider it too dangerous for him to travel by train, so whenever he makes a trip, it is on his father's yacht, the *Standart*.

"On the decks of this big boat the little boy was supposed to be quite safe, as the officers and crew were devoted to him. He spent weeks at a time on the *Standart,* making cruises that took him far out to sea. Another yacht whose duty it was to protect the *Standart,* always sailed alongside the Czar's vessel, ready to go to its assistance at a moment's notice. With both yachts manned by men loyal to their ruler, it seemed that at last the Czar had found a place where he and his family could live in peace. And yet, one day when they were on a long cruise, the captain of the *Standart* headed the yacht for a channel known to be filled with submerged rocks. The guardian yacht immediately steamed away in another direction. The Czar, who was romping on deck with his children, failed to notice that the companion-boat had disappeared and that the

Standart was alone in the channel. Suddenly there was a terrible, grinding sound. The yacht, that had been going at top speed through this dangerous passage, came to a short stop. Water poured into its hold where its bottom had been ripped open by a rock. The Czar ordered the captain to signal the other yacht to come to the *Standart's* assistance. But the boat was out of sight and hearing. Lifeboats were lowered and the family taken off the yacht.

"This accident shook the Czar's faith in the captain's loyalty. It seemed that even a yacht, sailing in far-away waters, was not a safe refuge for the young Czarevitch. The family returned to the little palace at Tsarskoe Seloe. The Czarevitch was allowed less freedom than ever. He lives the life of a prisoner, although surrounded by luxuries. He has no playmates, excepting his sisters. All of his food is prepared by his mother or by an old cook who has been in the family for many years.

"When he plays in the palace grounds and in the nursery, he is guarded by a huge, black man who dresses in black and gold, and who was presented to the Czar many years ago by the Emperor of Abyssinia. The Czarevitch delights in being swung up to the black man's shoulders, there to sit astride his neck shouting, 'Hurrah!' at the top of his voice. It is his chief amusement.

"His grandmother objects to the way the little boy is being brought up. She says that his parents will make a girl of him, and she urges them to give him more freedom and to allow him to play with the little boys in the families of the Grand Dukes. But the Czarina shakes her head. She has learned that the life of a little Russian Czarevitch is in constant danger, so little Alexis is almost never allowed out of her sight.

"Of course, finding so much treachery all about her, has saddened the life of the Czarina, who as a girl, was surrounded by faithful friends and a loving family. And now, little Katrinka, that is all I can tell you tonight. Your eyes are growing heavy and Peter is already asleep. To-morrow, long before you are up, I shall have left the house. It may be that I shall not come back to-morrow night. However, I shall leave word with the housekeeper to look after you and Peter, and shall ask the good man downstairs, who plays in the orchestra at the Imperial Theater, to see that no harm comes to you."

Katrinka sprang to her feet and clasped the arm of Stefan Norvitch.

"I am afraid," she said. "You speak as if you were going far away like our father and mother, Stefan Norvitch. Surely, you would not go away and leave Peter and me so soon after we had found you."

"Strange things happen in Russia, Katrinka. But I shall make arrangements for the future of you and Peter, so that if some night I do not return to you, I can rest happy in the thought that Peter Petrovski's children are being cared for."

He rose, crossed the floor and laid Peter on the couch near the window. Then he undressed the child, wrapped him in a great woolly robe and covered him with a blanket.

"There is a little room at the end of the hall, Katrinka, and in it a small bed. It is the room where your father slept when he was with me. It shall be yours now."

He laid his great hand on Katrinka's head. "Good night, little one."

Katrinka reached up and seized his hand, kissing its fingers after the Russian custom.

"Good night, Stefan Norvitch," she said, raising her eyes to an ikon [22] that hung at the end of the room. Then, releasing his big hand, she crossed herself with her thumb and two first fingers, went softly down the hall and entered the room that had been her father's. In the corner stood a tiny, white bed.

Tears sprang to Katrinka's eyes. She ran to the bed and, throwing herself on her knees beside it, kissed the hard pillow.

"Oh, little pillow," she whispered, "I love you, because upon you a dear head has rested."

CHAPTER XX

KATRINKA SEES A PARADE

WHEN Katrinka awoke in the morning, Stefan Norvitch had already breakfasted and left the house. Katrinka was disappointed, and although the housekeeper set before her the half of a delicious cucumber on which honey had been thickly spread, Katrinka had little appetite.

After breakfast she went downstairs to ask the old musician to direct her to Stefan Norvitch's shop. She longed to see the place where her father had worked.

"The shop is closed to-day," said the old man, putting down the accordeon on which he was playing. "Stefan Norvitch has joined the workingmen's parade. They are going to the Winter Palace in the hope of seeing the Czar, who is in St. Petersburg. Stefan Norvitch will make a speech. I am going to see the parade and will take you and your little brother with me if you wish it."

Katrinka was delighted. She remembered the parade of girls in the park in the village of Tsarskoe Seloe. She fancied that all parades were like that one.

"I will bring Peter at once," she said, running gayly upstairs to put on her kerchief.

"Oh, Peter," she cried, bursting into the room where he sat gravely looking at picture books, "we are going to have a holiday and see a parade. And perhaps we shall see the Little Father."

She tied a flowered handkerchief about her head, opened the sheet in which her clothes were still packed, took out a handsome apron that had belonged to her mother and that was embroidered in cross stitch, fastened it about her waist, took Peter by the hand and went downstairs.

The parade was already approaching when the old musician, leading Katrinka and Peter, arrived in front of the Winter Palace.

Katrinka looked at the long line of men wonderingly, her underlip between her teeth. Among the marchers there were no gayly dressed hussars with red trousers tucked into shining boots, and coats trimmed with gold braid. This parade was made up of shabby, pale-faced men in ragged clothing, some of them barefooted, all of them gaunt and hollow eyed, as if they had gone hungry for days. She had seen men in the village of Vachok who had looked like this at the end of winter. They had come to her father's house to ask for food. Some of them had walked from villages miles away. For days they had lived on the straw with which their houses were thatched, grinding it and mixing it with water. When the straw was all gone they had come to her father for help.

Katrinka had seen so many women in beautiful carriages driving about the streets in St. Petersburg, that she was surprised to discover that here, as in the village of Vachok, there were starving people. She looked up inquiringly at the old musician. But his eyes were fixed on the parade and when Katrinka spoke he merely said, "Hush, child," in a strange voice.

The parade stopped in front of the great Winter Palace. A few of the men took pipes from their pockets as if they expected they might have to wait some time for the appearance of the Czar. While they were lighting them there was the sound of galloping hoofs, and the next moment a body of Cossacks, mounted on beautiful little horses and wearing coats all trimmed with gold, dashed into the square in front of the Palace. Katrinka gasped in delight. It was going to be a beautiful parade after all. The next moment she covered her eyes with her hands.

There was a terrible rumble. The Cossacks had fired their guns into the midst of the working-men's parade. Confusion reigned. Men ran to and fro, shouting at the top of their voices. Women and children shrieked. Katrinka felt herself being jerked backwards by a rough hand on her arm. She uncovered her eyes. The old musician whirled Peter up from the sidewalk and, still holding Katrinka's hand, started down the street as fast as he could go.

Again and again there was the terrible rumbling sound, followed by shrieks. Katrinka shouted to the old musician.

"They are shooting Stefan Norvitch," she cried. "Let us run back and help him. I saw him. There was blood on his face and he was stretching his arms towards us. Then he fell. Oh, please, let us go back and help him."

The musician paid no attention to her words. He seemed panic-stricken. Women with babies in their arms and other children dragging at their skirts, half-grown boys and girls, and now and then one of the pale-faced working-men who had taken part in the parade, were one and all hurrying through the streets at top speed.

It was not until the old musician was within a block of home that he stopped his breathless flight, and for the first time realized that Katrinka was begging him to turn back.

"Tut, tut, my child," he said, looking over his shoulder fearfully. "We can do no good there. The thing for us to do is to get under shelter as soon as possible. When the Cossacks begin an attack there is no telling where they will stop."

"But why did they shoot Stefan Norvitch?" gasped Katrinka, breathlessly. "He was a good man."

"I know—I know. But he was in the parade. Our police—the guards at the Winter Palace—are panic stricken when they hear of a parade. They fancy that an army is about to march upon Tsarskoe Seloe and destroy the whole royal family. The Cossacks are ordered out. You have seen the result."

Katrinka looked up at the old musician. His face was very white. She could feel his fingers trembling.

"You are shivering," she said. "Are you afraid?"

The man did not answer. He hurried along the street, and presently, with Katrinka and Peter, entered his little apartment on the ground floor of the house where Stefan Norvitch lived.

CHAPTER XXI

KATRINKA MAKES A NEW FRIEND

TWO weeks passed. Still Katrinka heard nothing from Stefan Norvitch. She and Peter lived in his apartment, but they found it lonely in spite of its books and pictures. Sometimes in the afternoons they ventured into the streets, but the sight of a man in uniform would send them running back to shelter.

It was after one of these excursions that Katrinka, returning to the house, saw a handsome carriage, drawn by three black horses, standing in front of the door. The thought flashed through her mind that the little Grand Duchess, Tatiana, had found her out and had come to see her. She hurried upstairs, opened the door of Stefan Norvitch's apartment and looked eagerly around. There was nobody there excepting the old housekeeper who continued to come every day just as she had done before Stefan Norvitch went away.

"Has a little girl wearing a black velvet coat and a velvet cap been here while Peter and I were walking?" shouted Katrinka into the woman's ear.

The housekeeper shook her head.

"But there is a carriage outside with three horses, and the driver has on a red coat trimmed with gold. I think the Grand Duchess, Tatiana, must be in the house somewhere."

The housekeeper shrugged her shoulders. "A prince lives on the floor above us. He has a great many visitors who come in carriages."

Katrinka looked surprised. She did not know that in the city of St. Petersburg it is not unusual for the upper floors of a house to be occupied by noblemen, although families of very plain people live on the floors below. Still hoping that Tatiana had come to see her, she resolved to go downstairs and ask the old musician if he had seen the little girl.

She found the old man playing on his accordeon. The door stood open and Katrinka entered softly. The music was slow and very sad. Katrinka listened to it for some time.

The hope of seeing Tatiana faded. She thought of her father and mother in far-away Siberia. Again she saw the parade of working-men. She clasped her hands against her breast and, raising her face, began to dance, telling her story in the rhythmical movement of her feet and body.

The old musician, who had played for hundreds of Russian dancers, looked at the child, astonished. But he continued playing, while Katrinka danced, gravely at first, then, as the melody changed, beating time to it, joyously, as she had done that day in the park at Tsarskoe Seloe.

Neither the man nor the child noticed that a woman in a trailing gown of mauve-colored satin had descended the stairs and stopped in the doorway to watch Katrinka. The music grew faster and faster, and in time with it Katrinka leaped and whirled, waving her arms like a bird beating the air with its wings.

Finally, the music ended and Katrinka, with a final pirouette on her toes, stopped dancing, and her eyes rested for the first time on the handsomely gowned woman who now stepped from the shadowy hall into the light of the room. With an embarrassed exclamation, Katrinka shrank into the corner. But the woman continued to advance, and approaching the child, laid a hand on her shoulder.

"You should be in the Imperial school for dancers," she said. "Your little feet and your gestures are wonderful. Is the child your daughter?"

She turned towards the old musician, who threw out his hands apologetically.

"No, Your Ladyship. She is a little peasant girl who came from the village of Vachok to see Stefan Norvitch who was shot in the parade of working-men. I did not know until to-day that the child had wings on her feet."

"You speak correctly—the little one has, indeed, winged feet. She should be trained for the Imperial ballet. Where are her parents? I will get their permission to put the child in the Czar's school for dancers."

"My father and mother are in Siberia," explained Katrinka, looking wistfully into the face of the woman. Her cheeks were glowing, her little breast was heaving, her breath came from her parted lips in gasps. The dance had exhausted her. The woman studied her through narrowed eyelids. She had stepped back as Katrinka finished speaking. Now she approached the child again, smiling. Katrinka looked at her, wondering where she had seen her before. It was as if a half-forgotten friend had unexpectedly appeared before her.

"That is unfortunate," said the stranger. "The Czar may object to having in the school a child whose parents are exiled. With what crime are your parents charged, little one?"

Katrinka's underlip quivered. "My father and mother are very good people. They loved the Czar. Ivan Drovski said that they were sent away because father had a printing-press and tried to teach his neighbors to read."

"Poor child! You seem to be another victim of our mistaken form of government. It may be that I can help your parents, but for the time being we will not discuss that matter. I should make myself very unpopular at the court if I attempted to get a pardon for your parents just now. I lost favor when I pleaded for the release of my own brother. Later on —who knows? I have some powerful friends. I will speak to them."

She threw the shimmering scarf, that she carried on her arm, over her shoulders and turned to the musician.

"May I take the child, just as she is, to the Imperial ballet school? One of the greatest masters in St. Petersburg is there at this hour. I should like to have him see this little girl dance and give me his opinion. Unless I am greatly mistaken, she has a wonderful future before her."

"You may take the child if she is willing to go with you," said the musician. The woman turned to Katrinka, holding out her hand

"Will you come with me?" she asked. "My carriage is outside."

Katrinka shook her head shyly.

"I could not go without Peter."

"Peter?" exclaimed the woman. "Who is Peter?"

"He is my little brother. He is taking a nap in Stefan Norvitch's arm-chair. Would you like to see him?"

A laugh, that sounded to Katrinka like the soft tinkling of bells, came from the woman's lips. She took the child's hand.

"I should be happy, indeed, to see your little brother. Take me to him."

Side by side they went up the stairs. Katrinka softly pushed open the door leading into Stefan Norvitch's study. Peter was sitting up in the big chair rubbing his eyes. He had grown plump and rosy. Katrinka pointed to him proudly.

"That is my little brother. I pray every night that he will not grow up either a man of letters or of the sword. When he gets big I should like to have him a woman, or a farmer like Ivan Drovski, so that he may be safe from the Cossacks."

Again the woman's laugh rippled across her lips.

"Even a woman is not always safe from the Cossacks, my child," she said, as Peter slipped from his chair and half hiding behind Katrinka's skirt, stared at their visitor, his chubby forefinger in his mouth. The woman looked at a jeweled watch that hung from a chain about her neck. "It is getting late," she said. "Put on your hat, child. We must start for the Imperial ballet school at once."

"I—I have only a kerchief," stammered

Katrinka, her eyes on the wonderful hat made entirely of violets that the woman was wearing.

"All the better," said the woman with a reassuring smile. "But we must make haste. Come, little brother, we are going to have a ride."

"Hurrah," cried Peter, forgetting his bashfulness and dashing towards the door.

Katrinka tied her kerchief over her head.

"What is your name, child?" asked the woman, "and your age?"

"My name is Katrinka Petrovna," replied Katrinka, using the new name. "I am ten years old."

"You are old enough then to enter the school, and so clever that you will have no difficulty in passing the examinations."

When they reached the street they found the coachman scolding Peter roundly for having attempted to get up beside him. The man looked abashed when his mistress appeared, leading Katrinka by the hand, and asked him to lift the little boy into the carriage.

A moment later the horses galloped away, the bell over the middle horse clanging, the

silver trappings on the harness jingling musically.

After a ride through many strange and interesting streets, the carriage drew up with a
flourish before a large but gloomy building.
The strange woman in the satin gown descended and held out one of her tiny gloved
hands to Katrinka, who took it shyly.

"Give your other hand to little brother," she
said, pushing a bell in the wall of the building.

In response to her ring, the upper part of
a heavy door opened, and Katrinka saw a large
man, wearing a blue suit trimmed with brass
buttons. He glanced at her companion who
gave him a card. Then, forthwith, he opened
the rest of the door and ushered the strange
party into a softly lighted room. Its walls
were covered with pictures of girls whose
skirts stood out around them like the leaves of
a full-blown rose, and of men in a variety of
strange costumes.

Katrinka was studying the pictures wonderingly, when a long, thin man entered. Immediately he and the strange woman began to
talk very rapidly in a language that Katrinka

did not understand. She knew that they were talking about her, for the man turned abruptly every few minutes to look at her sharply.

"Madame Morenski says that you can dance." He hunched his shoulders and raised his eyebrows doubtingly. "Every day or two, some delightful but mistaken woman brings me an infant prodigy."

He scowled and shook his head. "Their ducks are all swans. But, come, I will see what you can do."

Katrinka's knees trembled beneath her. Her face flushed. Her heart seemed to be pounding like a little engine in her throat. She cast an appealing glance at Peter, who, as if understanding her fear, slid down from his chair and ran to her side.

"I'll fight you with my sword," he said, frowning at the man. He pulled Katrinka towards the door leading to the street. But she held back. She longed to run away, but something in the man's face restrained her. In spite of his words and his abrupt manner, she detected a kind gleam in his eyes, and his thin lips quivered into a smile at Peter's words.

"Do not be afraid, child. Hundreds of

children, no older than you, have danced for
me. In five minutes I will know whether or
not you have any talent, let alone the genius
which Madame Morenski claims for you.
Come."

He led the way into a great, dusky room
with a stage at the end of it. Below, in front
of the stage, a man was slipping a case over his
violin. Another sat before a piano. Several
others seemed about to leave. The thin man
shouted to them.

A few moments later Katrinka was listening to melodies that she had heard hundreds
of times in the village of Vachok, and to which
the boys and girls of the village danced. But
never before had the music seemed so sweet
and beautiful. She clasped her hands upon
her breast. Homesick tears filled her eyes.
The man approached her, held out his hand,
bent down and spoke to her in a low voice.

"Come, let us dance, little one," he said.

He led her to the middle of the stage, taking
a few of the steps of the Russian Peasant's
dance; and Katrinka, forgetting her fears, began to dance as she had danced in the park at

Tsarskoe Seloe and again in the room of the old musician.

In the wings leading from the stage, the lady in the violet hat stood holding Peter's hand. Her eyes were fixed wonderingly upon Katrinka, who, in her brown peasant dress with the kerchief tied over her head, her slender arms outstretched, her little feet beating time more and more swiftly to the familiar strains of the folk songs which she had heard and loved since her babyhood, looked like some strange brown bird that had fluttered by mistake into the dim, old theater.

When at last the music stopped, the dancing master, who had long since left Katrinka's side and retired into the shadows where he stood with folded arms watching the child, stepped nimbly to the side of the woman in the wings.

"You were right about this little girl, Madame. She has talent. I can do something with her if she is strong enough to stand the training."

While the master was speaking, Katrinka had approached and now stood with her arm about Peter. Her face was flushed, her eyes filled with wonder. For years, unheeded, she had gone up and down the dusty street that ran through the village of Vachok, dancing and singing Russian songs. It seemed strange that the dancing which had attracted no attention in her native village should assume so much importance, first in Tsarskoe Seloe where the Czar himself had sent her a capful of silver, and now in St. Petersburg, where six grown men had been ordered to take out their instruments and play, in order that one little girl in a peasant's dress and bark sandals might dance.

For a long time after the music had stopped, the man and the woman talked with each other. Then the woman gave her hand to Katrinka.

"Come," she said, "I will drive you home now. Everything will be arranged. You are to become a pupil at the Imperial Institute. But before you can be admitted to the dancing classes you must pass some examinations in reading, writing and geography. It will no doubt be a year before you have learned to read well enough—"

"Father taught me to read long ago," interrupted Katrinka, and then blushed at her rudeness.

"You know how to read?" exclaimed Madame Morenski, opening her eyes. "That will help a great deal."

"Oh, yes," replied Katrinka. "Even little Peter can read. He and I had lessons every day until father and mother were taken away."

Madame Morenski looked pleased. "That is good," she said. "Very few of the young girls who apply for places in the school can read. Almost none of them have studied history and geography. In order to teach them these branches there is a preparatory school supported by the Czar, to which the applicants go for one and, sometimes, two years before they are allowed to enter the dancing school. Each autumn the pupils from this school are examined and if the result is satisfactory they are passed into the Ballet Institute. To-morrow I am again to see the master who saw you dance to-day. He will arrange a private examination for you. If you pass it a governess will be engaged to visit you every day to teach you the things you must know before taking the tests which admit you to the dancing school, if passed in a satisfactory way." She paused, her eyes on Peter. "I must also provide for the little brother's future," she said, a frown puckering her forehead. "Perhaps I can get him into one of the government schools."

She smiled, then, as when they had come, took each child by the hand. They passed from the theater into the fresh out-door air where the carriage was waiting.

CHAPTER XXII

ON the following Monday, Madame Morenski again visited the house of Stefan Norvitch. She found Katrinka baking spice cakes under the direction of the old housekeeper, a huge gingham apron covering her from neck to feet.

"Oh," cried Madame Morenski, gayly, "I must have made a mistake. I came this morning to see a little ballet dancer. Instead I find a young cook. Will you tell me please where Mademoiselle Petrovna lives?"

Katrinka laughed and made a curtsey. Then she unfastened the great apron. "Ah, you are she," exclaimed Madame Morenski, pretending to be very much surprised. "Let us sit on a bench near the oven where we can watch the spice cakes while I tell you of all that has happened since I last saw you."

Katrinka looked from Madame Morenski's

beautiful violet gown to the rude bench. Madame Morenski noticed her troubled expression, smiled brightly and immediately perched herself on the bench.

"My cook at home is a very cold and ungracious person," she said. "I am never allowed in her kitchen and, as there is nothing in the world that I like better to eat than hot spice cakes, I shall sit here until they are done and then I shall eat—oh, three at least. Come and sit beside me, Peter, and you, too, Katrinka. I am impatient to tell you what the master says of your dancing." Katrinka lifted Peter to the bench, then climbed up beside him. Madame Morenski cuddled the little boy against her.

Peter reached up and patted her cheek. "Matusia," he whispered softly, and lifting his eyes demanded: "Have you a little boy at your house?"

Madame Morenski sighed. "No," she replied.

"Poor, pretty lady," murmured Peter. "Who takes care of you?"

"Nobody."

"Are you afraid?"

"Sometimes."

Peter sighed. "I cannot go to your house to live because Katrinka is afraid, too, and I must stay with her. Perhaps, if you are good, I can find a little boy without any sister, who will take care of you."

"Thank you," said Madame Morenski as Peter again nestled his head against her shoulder. "Now, Katrinka, I will tell you some good news."

Katrinka leaned forward, her eyes eager, her cheeks flushed.

"The master says you have talent," went on Madame Morenski. "He has arranged for the committee in charge of the Institute for Dancers to give you a special examination to-morrow morning at ten o'clock. If you pass this you will become a regular member of the dancing school where you will be taught, not dancing alone, but many, many other things, among them French, German and music, and all at the expense of the Czar."

Katrinka clasped her hands delightedly. "Oh, how very good the Little Father is," she cried.

Madame Morenski's blue eyes clouded.

"You are a fortunate little one, Katrinka. In our country it is usually difficult for a poor child to get even an ordinary education. But you have a great gift. It sets you apart from other little girls. In Russia dancing is considered one of the arts and is fostered like music and painting. A child who proves to have real talent for dancing is given many advantages and receives as thorough an education as the little Grand Duchesses, the daughters of the Czar." She paused, then leaned forward and smiled into Katrinka's upturned face. "I shall come for you at ten o'clock tomorrow morning to take you to the Institute where the examinations will be held. But the spice cakes are done. Let us take them up."

They turned the spice cakes upon a square of white linen while the housekeeper lighted the samovar. Half an hour later Madame Morenski bade the children good-by and drove away.

The following morning at ten o'clock Katrinka, clinging to the hand of her new friend, her heart fluttering like an imprisoned bird, appeared at the Ballet Institute for her examination. She and Madame Morenski were shown into the director's office where they had barely seated themselves when the door opened and Katrinka heard her name called. She sprang to her feet, then turned towards Madame Morenski.

"Do they want us?" she asked.

"They want you, Katrinka," explained Madame Morenski. "I will wait here for you."

Again Katrinka heard her name called. She cast Madame Morenski a frightened farewell glance, then, with knees trembling, followed the man who had spoken her name, into a great bare hall with mirrors set in the walls, and a huge round table at one end about which several men were seated.

Katrinka was told to walk up and down before the table. Then she was asked to jump over several obstacles, to lift one knee and then the other, to bend her body from side to side. To her surprise she was not asked to dance. Instead, she was presently taken into another room where a kind faced old gentleman tested her heart and her lungs. Then she was given a book and asked to read from it, and later to point out various cities on a map that hung on the wall. At the end of the examination she was again taken to the outer room where Madame Morenski was waiting.

With Madame Morenski was the master who had seen Katrinka dance. As she entered the room he came to meet her, holding out his hand.

"I have been thinking of you, my child. I have great hopes for your future. But you must work. You must grow in gentleness and grace, in lightness and harmony. Then, if you pass the examinations, some day, within the coming year, I may allow you to dance for the Czar and Czarina. How would you like that?"

For a moment Katrinka could not answer. Her heart seemed to be beating in her throat. Her temples throbbed so loudly that she fancied the master must hear them. She clasped her hands against her breast.

"Oh, sir, you ask how I would like to dance for the Czar and the Czarina? Why, that means everything to me. I could tell them how lonely Peter and I have been without our father and mother and how happy we should be to have them returned to us again."

The master's eyes sparkled. "Ah," he said.

"So it is the story of your own sorrow that you were telling me the other day when you danced. It was like the singing of a nightingale—heartbreaking. I did not understand it. My eyes misted." He turned to Madame Morenski. "Madame," he went on, "I cannot thank you enough for bringing this child to me. Already she knows the dance language."

Madame Morenski took Katrinka's hand. "I am glad that you are pleased with the child," she said. "I, too, believe that she has a great future as a dancer. Good morning."

A few days later Katrinka received word that she had passed her examinations and that she would be permitted to enter the Ballet Institute in the fall. Meantime she would be given special instruction in music and French.

During the remainder of the summer she would be permitted to live in the house with Stefan Norvitch's housekeeper, but when she entered the regular dancing class she would become a ward of the Czar. From that time on she would have to live in the school with the other pupils.

This troubled Katrinka, who wondered what would become of little Peter. Madame Morenski reassured her by explaining that plans were already under way to place him in a government school for boys.   She promised that Katrinka should be allowed to see him as often as once in two weeks.

CHAPTER XXIII

THE next morning, while Katrinka slept, dreaming that she was again dancing along the single, winding street in the village of Vachok, the little Imperial Prince Alexis, in the palace at Tsarskoe Seloe, was wrinkling his small nose in disgust over his porridge.

Beside him sat his mother, the Empress of all the Russias, dressed simply in a morning gown of lavender linen, her hair wound in a soft coil around her head. There was a worried line between her eyebrows as she urged the little Alexis to eat his porridge.

"Tatiana and Olga are having nice little pancakes with sugar on them for their breakfast," he said, pushing away the silver bowl in which the porridge steamed.

"Pancakes with sugar on them are not as good for little boys as oatmeal porridge," said the Empress, smiling into the troubled eyes of

217

her small son. "But if you will eat your porridge this morning, I may make some little pancakes for your breakfast to-morrow."

Little Alexis dipped his spoon into the porridge. "I will try to eat it," he said.

The Czarina leaned back in her chair with a sigh of relief. She had learned to cook years ago when she was a young girl in the village of Darmstadt, and in those days she was famous for her delicious cakes and salads. Then she married the Czar of Russia, and after that time she lived in the midst of so much pomp and ceremony that the simple accomplishment of her girlhood was forgotten.

But the birth of the Czarevitch, and the plots against his life which followed, made it necessary for her again to take up the homely tasks which she had laid aside so many years ago. She had a little kitchen fitted up, opening into the family dining room in the palace at Tsarskoe Seloe. Here, a big apron tied around her waist, assisted by an old cook who has been in the family for many years, she prepares all of the food that her small son eats. Sometimes, like more humble cooks, she scorches the toast or fails to season the porridge to his taste. On these occasions the little Alexis finds fault quite frankly with his royal mother.

When it became known among the friends of the Czarina that she had ordered a kitchen fitted up for her especial use, they shrugged their shoulders and raised their eyebrows disdainfully.   But the lovely Czarina, who is mistress of hundreds of servants and of many, many palaces, pays no heed to them.   She performs her homely tasks with sweetness and patience, striving with all her might once more to become an accomplished cook for the sake of her small son.

When, on this particular morning, the little Czarevitch had finished his porridge, he slipped from his high chair and ran to a window looking out upon the terraces, where two little girls, dressed alike in plain white frocks, their hair brushed back from their foreheads and tied on the crown of their heads with bows of white ribbon, were playing by the fountain.

"I see Tatiana and Olga," he cried.   "May I go out and play with them?"

"If you will not go out of sight of my sitting

room windows," began his mother, then looked up as a small, dark-bearded man entered the room. It was the Czar.

Immediately the little Alexis forgot all about his sisters. He darted across the room and into the outstretched arms of his father, who tossed him into the air, then turned to the Czarina.

"I shall have to go to St. Petersburg this afternoon," he said, holding out a telegram which he carried in his hand.

The Czarina's eyes clouded. "For how long, Nica," she asked, calling her husband by the pet name she had given to him during the days of their courtship.

"For two days at least," he replied.

"You will be lonely."

"Yes," he sighed. In the days before the birth of little Alexis he seldom went to the city without taking the Czarina with him, but since the many attempts against the life of their son, the Czarina has given up making trips with her husband.

"Why not take Olga and Tatiana with you? They have not been to St. Petersburg for a long time," suggested the Czarina as the two girls, spying their father from a distance, came running across the terrace.

"I was thinking of that very thing," he replied as they entered the room. "How would you like a trip to St. Petersburg," he went on, turning towards them.

"With you?" they exclaimed in one breath.

"Yes."

"It would make us very happy," cried Tatiana, flashing a smile at her father.

"Indeed it would," added Olga; then looked suddenly grave. "But to-morrow is Marie's birthday. Perhaps we ought to stay at home and celebrate it with her."

The Czarina shook her head. "I will take Alexis, Anastasia and Marie for a picnic on the island. Alexis is old enough now to be told how his great-grandfather, Alexander II, and his brothers built the little stone house there, and laid out the entire garden, while still little boys."

Olga looked from her father to her mother, as if undecided whether to stay at home and go on the picnic with her mother, or to go up to St. Petersburg with her father. She was very fond of visiting the island in one of the larger lakes of Tsarskoe Seloe, and she never tired of playing in the stone house that her great-grandfather had built there many, many years ago. He and his brothers had also made the furniture in the little cottage, as well as a fortress where they played war-games, sometimes defending it, and sometimes attacking it.

The Czar caught the expression on his older daughter's face.

"Remain at home, if you wish, Olga," he said, considerately. "I shall be busy all day to-morrow, but I thought you might enjoy a shopping excursion with one of your governesses."

"Indeed I should," said Olga. "If mother takes Marie to the island for her birthday, she will not miss Tatiana and me."

"And there is a new music-box in the museum," added Tatiana. "And dozens of baby canaries will be hatching out now. Do you remember them last summer, Olga, and how we fed them with bread and milk?"

"Yes, and how very large their beaks were," replied Olga, linking her arm into Tatiana's and following their parents into the nursery where Alexis and their two younger sisters.

who had breakfasted half an hour earlier, were coasting on the slippery toboggan-slide that had been set up in the center of the big, airy room. As they entered the room Alexis was coming down the slide like the wind, his fair hair blown back from his forehead, his cheeks glowing with excitement. Behind him, her arms around his waist, sat little Marie, the youngest of the Czar's daughters, who has always been so good that Olga claims that she must be an adopted child, as it is unnatural for one of the children to be so much more docile and good-natured than the others.

"Oh, Alexis!" cried Tatiana, helping him to his feet, "Olga and I are going to St. Petersburg this afternoon with father."

"So am I," replied Alexis, clinging to Tatiana's hand.

"Oh, no, Alexis. You cannot go this time," explained Olga. "Only Tatiana and I are going."

Alexis flung his sister's hand from him. "You are a naughty girl, Olga, and shall not have any supper." He ran to Tatiana and taking her hand in his, looked up into her face winningly.

"Olga shall stay at home," he said, "and Tatiana and I will go to St. Petersburg with father."

For a moment Tatiana did not reply. It is necessary for the other children to treat the little Czarevitch with a great deal of consideration. He has had his own way so much that he is a very self-willed and spoiled little boy in spite of his sweet face and usually pretty manners.

Tatiana, realizing that a storm was threatening, immediately began talking about the picnic that was being planned for the next day. Alexis presently forgot all about the trip to St. Petersburg, and Olga and Tatiana slipped from the nursery a few minutes later and ran upstairs to get ready for their journey.

Just before noon a small party, consisting of the Czar, the two little girls, the German governess and several guards, left Tsarskoe Seloe. Word had already been sent out that the Czar was about to make a journey, and before he stepped on board the train a messenger assured one of his attendants that every mile of track between Tsarskoe Seloe and St. Petersburg had been carefully inspected and special guards stationed along the route.

After reaching St. Petersburg the party was driven to the Winter Palace and the children hurried at once to the aviary where dozens of canaries flit among the palms.

"We are too early," said Tatiana, disappointedly. "Nearly every nest has a mother bird on it. The eggs have not yet hatched. Let us come back here to-morrow after we have finished our shopping. We will spend this afternoon in the museum and the play-room."

"Very well," replied Olga. "One of papa's friends has just sent him a new writing-table with a music-box concealed in it. Let us see if we can discover how to start it." She linked her arm in her sister's and turned to the German governess, who was listening to the singing of a beautiful yellow canary.

"We are going into the museum, Fraülein, to see the new music-box."

The governess joined her charges, who strolled leisurely through the great, white ball-room and crossed the state dining room. It was the first time that the governess had visited the Winter Palace, and Olga and Tatiana patiently pointed out the interesting things in the various rooms. In each, several sight-seers escorted by guides were moving about, for the public is allowed to visit all of the rooms of state at the palace, the living-rooms alone being private.

In one of the rooms the walls are covered with gold plates, many of them engraved with the monograms of Emperors long since dead, and inset in precious stones with the double-headed eagle that appears on Russian flags.

"Before father was ruler," explained Tatiana, pointing to the array of plates, "whenever the Czar entered a town, one of the headmen met him and presented him with bread and salt arranged on a beautiful, golden plate. It was a very pretty way of showing that they were glad to see their Czar. In some of the smaller villages the people were too poor to buy golden plates for him and so they had to present the bread and salt on ordinary china ones. This made them unhappy because, you see, the poor villagers were as pleased to see the Czar as the richer ones, although they could not afford to buy him such beautiful plates. So when papa came to the throne, he issued a decree that the bread and salt should be presented only on china or wooden dishes. So now, the gifts from the poor villages are as handsome as those from the rich ones. It was very thoughtful of him, I think."

"Yes," agreed Olga, "but papa is always like that. Everybody in the Empire must love him devotedly."

The German governess sighed and felt a twinge of pity for the two little girls. She realized that a very great many of the Czar's subjects not only do not love him, but wish him ill. She, herself, was very fond of him, having seen only the kind and loving side of the man, which he shows to his family. Like the children, she could not understand why all Russians were not loyal to their Czar.

A few moments later they entered the museum and Olga immediately discovered the writing-table with the concealed music-box. She knelt on the floor, looking everywhere for the secret spring that would start the mechanism, while Tatiana opened the drawers in the table, one after the other, suddenly crying out in delight as her eyes lighted upon a pearl knob.

She pressed the knob. Immediately the strains of a well-known melody filled the air. Olga sprang to her feet, and as she did so, almost collided with a party of sight-seers who had drawn near.

"I beg your pardon," she said prettily, stepping to one side, while Tatiana stood for a moment looking into the face of a little girl who was one of the new arrivals. Then her lips parted and she flashed a smile of recognition at the newcomer.

"Why," she said, "you are the little girl who dropped the samovar in front of our horses, are you not?"

The newcomer nodded. "Yes, I am Katrinka Petrovna," she said, drawing nearer.

Tatiana stepped back. There was a surprised expression in her eyes which swept from the top of Katrinka's head upon which was perched a Tam o' Shanter of blue velvet, to her feet in shining, new, kid slippers.

"And this is my little brother, Peter. You remember him—" went on Katrinka, pointing to Peter who stood nearby, clinging to the hand of Stefan Norvitch's old housekeeper.

"Oh, yes," said Tatiana, "but—" she paused,

looking wonderingly from one child to the other.

"I have been hoping to see you every day," said Katrinka, throwing out her hands with an eager gesture. "I wanted to tell you about our father and mother. They are in—" before she could finish the sentence the German governess had taken Tatiana by the arm.

"Do you know who these children are, Tatiana?" she asked severely.

"Yes, Fraülein," Tatiana answered, turning again towards Katrinka who opened her mouth as if to go on with her story, just as a guard hurried up and laid his hand on her shoulder.

"Come, come. No loitering," he said, roughly.

Katrinka looked appealingly towards Tatiana.

"My mother and father are in Siberia," she cried. "Peter and I beseech you to ask your father—" The guard pushed her forward. She glanced back. Tatiana was shrinking against the German governess. A frown darkened Olga's forehead.

"Papa will be angry, Tatiana, when I tell him that you have been talking with a stranger," said Olga reprovingly. "The little girl said that her father and mother were in Siberia. They must be very bad people who wish to do poor papa harm. Let us leave the museum—it is always full of sight-seers and strangers."

"Yes," said the governess severely. "Let us hurry back to the private rooms. Nobody knows what will happen next."

The mention of Siberia seemed to have sent a chill over the little party from Tsarskoe Seloe and as Katrinka looked over her shoulder in the vain hope that Tatiana had followed to hear more about her father and mother, she saw them disappearing behind a group of palms without even a parting glance.

Tears rose to Katrinka's eyes. Ever since morning she had been feeling strange and uncomfortable in the city clothes which Madame Morenski had sent to her. On the following day her lessons were to begin and in the autumn —Katrinka forgot the uncomfortable new clothes, the tears dried in her eyes. In the autumn, if she passed the examinations, she would enter one of the classes in the Czar's dancing school.

CHAPTER XXIV

THE FAVORITE SONG OF THE GRAND DUCHESSES

IMMEDIATELY after luncheon, Tatiana and Olga, in charge of their German governess, started on their shopping trip. They ate their luncheon in a small dining room not far from the nursery.

The first course was served at a little side table and the Czar, the children and their governess, ate it while standing. This course is called "Zakuska" [23] in Russia and is considered very important. It consisted of tiny, raw herrings arranged with pieces of lemon on a dainty platter, thin slices of bread spread with caviare, fresh radishes, small green onions sprinkled with Cayenne pepper, smoked salmon, salads, pickled mushrooms and various kinds of cheese.

In Russia, even the peasants begin their meals with the "Zakuska," which is supposed to give one a great appetite for the food that follows. The "Zakuska" of the poor people is, of course, very simple and frequently consists merely of a few pieces of black bread well sprinkled with vinegar and caraway seeds. But it is served on the prettiest plate that the house affords and in the houses of both the rich and the poor, it is eaten standing.

After nibbling at the various kinds of "Zakuska," the Imperial party went to the dining-table and ate what they considered a very delicious luncheon, beginning with cucumber soup with sour cream. The soup was followed by dumplings stuffed with chopped fish and cabbage. Then there was chicken and a salad made of hard-boiled eggs, beets, lettuce, chopped onion, radishes, capers, tomatoes, and celery, all smothered in a mayonnaise dressing. After the salad there was ice cream and fruit.

Olga and Tatiana enjoyed their luncheon, because it was thoroughly Russian. At their home in Tsarskoe Seloe the food is extremely simple, like the food that is served to children in England and America. Even the "Zakuska" is sometimes left out, for the Empress has never learned to enjoy the strange dishes that are served in this course, although the Czar is fond of them all, even of the pork "Zakuska" which is made of raw, sucking pig, chopped fine and sprinkled thickly with pieces of lemon and onion.

After luncheon the children started out to visit the shops. First of all, they went in search of a birthday present for little Marie. They had decided to get her a pair of roller skates, but they drove by the shops where skates were shown on the signboards, and finally stopped at a great store with large display windows like those in American cities. In front of it there was a lettered sign. These lettered signs are seldom seen in Russia. So few of the poor people can read or write that they would be useless, therefore all of the small shops have their fronts decorated with pictures of the wares sold within, painted in brilliant colors.

"We would better order at least twelve pairs of skates," said Olga, after she and Tatiana had explained to the salesman the kind of skates they wanted.

"Twelve pairs!" exclaimed the German governess, lifting her eyebrows in surprise.

"Marie is not a centipede. What will she do with twelve pairs of skates?"

"We must allow for the stealings," explained Olga. "It would do no good to buy a single pair of skates. They would disappear at once. It is always safest to buy at least a dozen of everything. Then we are sure of getting at least one thing for ourselves."

The governess shrugged her shoulders. She had heard about the stealings before, for it is well known in St. Petersburg that the greedy officials attached to the Russian court have a way of helping themselves to whatever they see fit, making life difficult for both the Czar and Czarina.

Their purchases completed, the party returned to the Winter Palace, where the governess lighted the samovar to heat the water for tea. After tea they all went to the nursery, a great room with crimson carpets and draperies, and with what the children called a mountain in the middle of the floor. This is used, like the slide at Tsarskoe Seloe, for indoor tobogganing.

"Let us slide down the mountain," said Olga, who felt lonely in the great Winter Palace and was already beginning to regret having come to St. Petersburg.

"Very well," replied Tatiana, running to the top of the slide. Olga watched her as she came spinning down, then turned to her governess with a sigh.

"There is no pleasure in tobogganing when there are only two of us," she said. "It is not exciting. Let us all sit down in the corner and play we are at home in Tsarskoe Seloe and that there are peacocks painted on the walls, like those in the nursery there."

"Oh, yes," cried Tatiana, joining her sister, "and we will play that this red room is a sun-shiny-yellow like the playroom at home. I can close my eyes and picture the walls there, with the daffodils in the border and the peacocks strutting about. Do you regret having come to St. Petersburg, Olga?"

Olga hesitated. "Father would have been lonely if we had remained at home. Perhaps if we all sing something beautiful we shall feel better. Can you think of a song, Tatiana?"

"Let us sing 'Villikens and His Dinah'—that is the nicest song I know. Will you begin it, please, Fraülein?"

Fraülein shook her head. "I never heard of the song," she explained.

"It is beautiful. We had an English governess who sang it to us. It was our favorite song. Tatiana and I will sing it for you. It is very sad."

The children put their arms about each other. Their voices blended sweetly as they sang the funny, old-fashioned English song, their little faces serious, their eyes fixed on the German governess, who found it difficult to keep a straight face.

VILLIKENS AND HIS DINAH [24]

There was a rich merchant in London did dwell,
Who had but one daughter, an uncommon fine **gal**:
Her name it was Dinah—just sixteen years old—
And she had a large fortune in silver and gold.

CHORUS

Sing too-ral, i-oo-ral, i-oo-ral, i-ay,
Sing too-ral, i-oo-ral, i-oo-ral, i-ay;
Sing too-ral, i-oo-ral, i-oo-ral, i-ay,
Sing a too-ral, i-oo-ral, i-ooral, i-ay.

As Dinah was walking the garden one day,
Her pah-pah came to her, and this he did **say,**

"Go dress yourself, Dinah, in gorgeous array,
And I'll bring you a husband, both gall-iant and gay."
CHORUS: etc.

"Oh! pah-pah, dear pah-pah," the maiden replied,
Just now to get marri-ed I don't feel inclined;
And all my large fortune, I'd gladly give o'er,
If I could remain single for a year or two more."

"Go! boldest of daughters," the par-i-ent rej'ined,
And if to get married, you don't feel inclined—
I'll give your large fortune to the nearest of kin,
And you shan't reap the benefit of one single pin."
CHORUS: etc.

As Villikens was walking the garden around,
He spied his dear Dinah lying dead on the ground;
And a cup of cold pisen was there by her side,
And a billy dux explaining 'twas of pisen she died.
CHORUS: etc.

He kissed her cold corpus a thousand time o'er—
And he called her his Dinah, though she wasn't not
     no more;
Then he drank up the pisen, like a lovyer so brave,
And Villikens and his Dinah both lay in one grave.
CHORUS: etc.

As the old man was a-walking the sights for to see,
He spied both their ghostses by a tall poplar tree:

And this they said to him—and they both looked quite
    blue—
"Oh, we shouldn't have been pisened, if it hadn't been
    for you."

CHORUS: etc.

Now, all you young ladies, take warning by her;
And, never not by no means, disobey your popp-er:
And all you young gentlemen, mind whom you clap-
    eyes-on—
Think of Villikens and his Dinah and the cup of cold
    pi'sen.

"Dear Miss Eager used to sing about Dinah
and her Villikens nearly every night," explained Tatiana when the song was finished
—then paused with a long-drawn sigh and
snuggled her cheek into the hollow of Olga's
shoulder.

"Yes," went on Olga, "we were very little
then, and sometimes Tatiana used to cry because she felt so sorry for Dinah."

"Because the poison was cold," explained
Tatiana, suddenly sitting up, and leaning towards Fraülein. "But, come, let us all go to
the theater."

"But it is too late for the matinée, and too
early for the evening performance," remon-

strated the governess, as both children sprang
from their seats delightedly.

"I know," explained Olga, putting on her
most grown-up manner, "we play make-believe
going to the theater; it is very amusing."

The children led the way through several
long corridors and finally arrived at the theater
of the Winter Palace. It was dark and de-
serted, save for two or three men who were
working about the stage, and a boy in uniform,
who was curled up in one of the orchestra
chairs half-asleep. As the children entered, he
sprang to his feet and saluted them politely.

"Will you please tell the stage-manager that
the Grand Duchesses Olga and Tatiana have
come, and ask him to let them see a play."

The boy dashed away, and a few minutes
later the theater was flooded with light and the
drop curtain lowered. Presently the boy in
uniform returned and ushered the children into
the Imperial box, with its hangings of crimson
velvet embroidered with the double-headed,
gold eagle, which one sees constantly in Russia.
The Russian flags show the eagle bearing the
blue cross of St. Andrew, and beneath there are
letters standing for Faith and Loyalty.

Olga and Tatiana settled into the comfortable chairs in the Imperial box, and the German governess, wondering what would happen next, sat down just behind them. The next moment the lights in the theater were turned out, and the drop curtain rolled up. Then followed scene after scene, as, one after another, the stage curtains were raised and lowered. The stage was empty, but that did not interfere with the delight of the children, who for years have played this game of make-believe theater when visiting at the Winter Palace. The old scene hands all know the little Grand Duchesses and are always willing to shift the scenery for their amusement.

CHAPTER XXV

THE following morning the little Grand
Duchesses were up early, and long before noon had finished their shopping. After
the last purchase had been made, their Fraülein
suggested returning at once to the Winter
Palace, but Olga insisted upon going to a tea-
house that she had once visited with her
mother. So the little party drove in the opposite direction from the palace, finally arriv-
ing at a pretty tea-house hung with bunches of
artificial wistaria.

They sat down in a tiny booth separated
from the rest of the shop by a green trellis, and
a dainty maid in a full, red skirt, blue bodice
and white apron, served them with glasses of
tea with slices of lemon floating on top. She
then passed a jar of jam and, to the surprise of
the German governess, each of the little Grand

241

Duchesses immediately stirred a spoonful of jam into her tea. Little cookies flavored with caraway and poppy seeds were then placed on the table, together with raspberries and strawberries heaped on green leaves, and a glass dish containing preserved pineapple.

The Grand Duchesses had barely finished their first glass of tea when Olga slipped off her chair.

"Let us leave here at once, Tatiana," she said decidedly. "That little girl who said that her father and mother were in Siberia has just entered the shop. She may blow us up."

The Fraülein glanced towards the front of the shop. There, indeed, stood Katrinka Petrovski, buying caraway cakes. As the little Grand Duchesses started towards the door she saw them, and turning towards them, would have spoken. But Tatiana threw back her head, glanced at Katrinka coldly and passed without speaking.

Tears rose to Katrinka's eyes. She could not understand the change in Tatiana. Then it suddenly occurred to her that probably the little Grand Duchess did not recognize her in her new dress and hat. She ran from the shop and, just as Tatiana was stepping into the carriage that waited outside, touched the sleeve of the little Grand Duchess.

"You do not know me," she began. "I am the little girl—"

A guard who had accompanied the children to the tea-house, and who stood beside the carriage, interrupted her words by pushing her roughly to one side. Tatiana glanced at Katrinka from the corner of her eye, then sprang into the carriage beside Olga. The guard jumped into the seat beside the driver who flourished his whip. The horses leaped forward.

"Isn't that the little girl whose parents were so wicked that poor papa had to send them to Siberia?" asked Olga. She did not realize that she had spoken loud enough for Katrinka to hear, but the clanking chains of the harness made so much noise that she had raised her voice and Katrinka heard quite plainly.

Through tear-dimmed eyes she watched the carriage until it disappeared. Then with a sigh she reëntered the tea-house and finished her purchases. As she walked slowly back to the house of Stefan Norvitch her mind was filled with misgivings. Like thousands of other children in Russia, she was beginning to understand what a chilling effect the mention of Siberia has upon the hearts of the Czar and his family.

When Olga and Tatiana reached Tsarskoe Seloe that evening, they found that the streets of the village were hung with flags and that nearly all of the shops were closed in honor of Marie's birthday.

It has been the rule ever since the Czar and his Czarina have made their home at the little palace in Tsarskoe Seloe, to celebrate the birthdays of their children by making them holidays, festive with flags.

Tatiana looked at the flags and then turned to her father.

"It is very pleasant to drive through the village where the people are so friendly. I wish everybody loved us the way they do in Tsarskoe Seloe and then it wouldn't be necessary to send people to prison in Siberia. It would be nice if we could live here forever and ever and never make visits to St. Petersburg. We should soon forget about the wicked people who wish to destroy us."

A frown darkened her father's forehead.

"Who has told you that there are people who wish to destroy us?"

"Nobody," replied Tatiana. "But I cannot help knowing because there are always guards about to protect us." Then her eyes grew wistful. "Do all children love their parents even when they are wicked, as we love you and mamma?" she asked.

"I suppose so," replied the Czar, smiling.

"They ought not to," said Olga suddenly. "When their parents are bad and are taken from them, the children should forget them and find new ones."

"That is what we are trying to do in our orphan asylums. We send the children there in order that they may be brought up properly and cared for."

"Oh!" exclaimed Tatiana, delightedly, clasping her hands. "Then the next time I see the little girl who walked from the village of Vachok and whose father and mother are in Siberia, I shall tell her to go to an orphanage and get some new parents."

"What do you mean, Tatiana?" demanded the Czar.

"A little girl came running up to us in the museum and told us that her parents were in Siberia," explained Olga. "We saw her again in the tea-house and she spoke to Tatiana again."

"Yes," said Tatiana, "I had seen her before. It was in the spring. She was on her way to the bazaar in the village of Tosna. She was with her little brother. They had walked a long distance and were very tired. We drove them to the bazaar."

"Who permitted you to do this?" demanded her father.

"Nobody. I asked the driver to put the children into the carriage. I did not know then that their parents were wicked people."

The Czar's face turned pale beneath its tan.

"Never again speak to a stranger, Tatiana," he said severely. Then he turned to their governess. "When you are out with any of the children, do not allow them to speak to strangers or to be spoken to by them."

Throughout the remainder of the drive he sat in silence, his lips compressed, his eyes serious.

On several occasions little children have been

sent to the Winter Palace with letters in which threats against the life of the Czar and his family have been made. There is no doubt that, as he drove through the peaceful village of Tsarskoe Seloe and entered the park surrounding the palace, the Czar wished as Tatiana had done, that he could remain quietly there for the remainder of his life among the villagers who love him.

When at last the carriage drew up before the palace entrance he drew a sigh of relief.

So many attempts have been made to take his life that the Czar has lost his courage. A word from one of his spies hinting that one of his subjects is laying a plot to destroy some member of the Imperial family, and that subject is sent post haste to prison without trial or warning.

CHAPTER XXVI

BLESSING THE ORCHARDS

AND now for Katrinka the weeks flew. It seemed to her that never before in her life had she been so busy as she was during these days. She passed the mornings with her music master or her French teacher and in the afternoons helped Stefan Norvitch's housekeeper with the sweeping and dusting.

When the late summer months came, and the days were followed by what are known in Russia as the "white nights," when darkness never settles down and midnight is almost as light as day, she and Peter took many walks after supper. Often they went far into the country along the road at the end of which, many miles away, was the village of Vachok.

On each side of the road were orchards enclosed by fences of wattled boughs. Now and then there were apple trees planted outside the

fences along the sides of the road.   The children watched the apples as they ripened and
many evenings sat under the boughs of one of
the largest of the wayside trees.   Sometimes
a rosy cheeked apple would fall to the ground,
almost at their feet.   They would look at it,
longingly, then push it away, for, as every Russian child will tell you, bad luck follows the
person who takes even a single bite from an
apple before the orchards have been blessed.

There was one beautiful apple that Peter
named for his own.   It hung high up in one of
the wayside trees.   Every evening when the
children walked in the twilight they stopped
under the tree bearing Peter's apple and gazed
up at it.

"Will the priest bless the orchards to-morrow?" Peter would ask.

"I hope so," Katrinka would reply, smooth-
ing his stiff, black hair.

"But how shall we know when the priest
comes?   Will he come in the evening so that
we can see him?"

"I do not know.   But if we do not see him
we shall know that the orchards have been

blessed because the people will be gathering the fruit."

"And perhaps some other little boy will climb up in the tree and get my apple," Peter would say. "Then what would I do?"

"There are other apples as big and rosy as yours. You may pick one of those."

Then Peter would shake his head stubbornly, and when at last the apples were so ripe that the air wafted the fragrance of the fruit to the children long before they could see the trees, Peter suggested their sleeping by the roadside to watch his apple.

But, as it happened, this was unnecessary. When the day for blessing the orchards finally arrived, Katrinka was given a holiday by her music master, who had a small estate just outside of St. Petersburg and was as anxious as little Peter to be on hand when his orchard was blessed.

That day the children left St. Petersburg early in the morning and stationed themselves under the wayside tree. Presently they saw the priest approaching. He had already blessed the orchards enclosed by the fences of wattled branches, and he would have passed by the wayside tree had not Katrinka hurried after him.

"Father," she cried, "there is a wayside tree that you have not blessed. Peter has chosen a fine apple in the top of it and we have a long stick hidden behind the fence with which I can reach it. Will you please come back and bless the tree so that I may get the apple for my little brother?"

The priest smiled good-naturedly and, turning back, stopped for a moment under the wayside tree to mutter the blessing. When he had done, Katrinka grasped his hand and kissed his fingers to show her gratitude.

"You may eat your fill of the fruit, my little ones," he said, seizing a branch of the tree and giving it a shake. "It will do you no harm now."

The following day all of the roads leading into St. Petersburg were filled with wagons loaded with apples from the orchards which had been blessed.

It was about a month after the blessing of the orchards that Katrinka went again to the Ballet Institute with Madame Morenski, for her second examination.

When she reached the Institute she found herself in the midst of a great number of children.

"Is it a party?" asked Katrinka, wonderingly.

Madame Morenski shook her head.

"No, these are the children from the preparatory school who, like you, have come to be examined by the officers of the Ballet Institute. There are a great many of them as you can see. Only a few of them will pass the examinations, and in case more of them pass than can be admitted to the classes, which are small, the directors will choose the most beautiful of the successful children and will turn away the others."

At these words Katrinka's heart sank. She looked from one to another of the little girls, anxiously waiting for the door of the big hall to be thrown open, then shook her head.

"Let us go back, Madame Morenski," she said. "I am not pretty like these other little girls. The directors will not want me. If my cheeks were red and round like Marie Drovski's it would be different."

"Round, red cheeks are not all that the examining board requires in the way of beauty, Katrinka," replied Madame Morenski. "Many times, girls with faces as pretty as those of dolls in shop windows are rejected, and plain little ones with intelligent expressions, chosen. Do not be disheartened, Katrinka."

As she finished speaking the doors of the great room, where the examinations were to take place, opened. The children filed into the hall, and almost immediately afterwards the tests began.

CHAPTER XXVII

IT was on the day following the first snow-
storm of the winter that Madame Morenski brought the news that Katrinka was one of
the ten applicants who had been accepted by
the examining board for the dancing classes.
Nearly two hundred children had been refused.

"Oh," cried Katrinka, her face radiant,
"then I shall soon dance again for the Czar.
I shall be one of the little children in his school
and can tell him all about father and mother,
and ask him to bring them home again."

Madame Morenski's face clouded. "I am
afraid you do not understand, Katrinka. Although the Czar is at the head of the Ballet
Institute, he sees the children only at a distance, at festivals and at special entertain-
ments. You will not be allowed to speak to
him and it will probably be a year before the

254

master will allow you to appear in public. Many months will pass before the Czar sees you. But keep a brave heart. You are about to begin a hard but interesting life. For the present you must forget your sorrows and think only of your work, which will begin in earnest in another week. To-day I have come to take you and Peter for a trip on the frozen river. Put on your warmest clothing and we will start at once."

At this announcement, Peter, who had just come into the room, clapped his hands, then threw his arms about Madame Morenski. He was so anxious to be off that he would hardly wait for Katrinka to button him into his new sheepskin coat and pull his fur cap over his ears. But at last they started, driving at once to the river.

As they reached its shore Katrinka cried out in delight. Never before had she beheld so gay a scene. The river was entirely frozen over, and hundreds of men and women, as well as boys and girls, were skating about on its surface, skimming over the ice, many of them taking dance steps. A great many pine trees had been cut and brought to St. Petersburg.

These had been set up on the river to form roads that seemed to be outlined with growing trees.

Pretty Madame Morenski left her sleigh and, giving a hand to Katrinka and Peter, walked to the end of one of these green lanes, waving her big muff to summon two boys on skates. A moment later the two children and the lovely young woman were seated in a green garden chair on runners and were being whisked across the river by the two boys who had responded to the summons.

They had almost reached the opposite shore when Katrinka noticed that everybody was looking towards an approaching sledge drawn by a small but swiftly trotting horse. In it was seated a man dressed like an ordinary general, an Astrachan cap on his head. Beside him sat a woman. Her large, sad eyes peered from beneath a small turban of fur. She was wrapped in a beautiful sable cape. The sledge was unattended save by a lackey in a green and pale-blue uniform, who rode on the low board in front.

It was not until Katrinka noticed that the police and sentries stationed along the route saluted the sledge as it passed, that she realized that the man and the woman who were driving along so quietly, were the Czar and Czarina of Russia. As she recognized them she felt a thrill run through her. She saluted them prettily as they dashed by, then rose to look after them. As the crowds on the river shut them from view she sank back with a sigh, then looked up into Madame Morenski's face. Madame Morenski smiled into her eyes, understandingly. Again Katrinka wondered where she had seen somebody who smiled like this kind, new friend. Madame Morenski, catching the puzzled expression in the child's eyes, which almost immediately gave way to a look of sadness, took one of Katrinka's hands and snuggled it into her great muff.

"Shake off your sadness, Katrinka," she said. "Grieving will not bring back your parents. Look about you, dear child. On every side there is gayety. And see—there is a sledge coming towards us, and in it are the Grand Duchesses, Tatiana and Olga."

Katrinka leaned forward. Her eyes sparkled, her cheeks were as red as winter apples. A dimple played at the corner of her mouth.

The heart-breaking sorrow that Madame Morenski had seen in her eyes a moment before had given way to a look of childish expectancy. Her gaze was fixed upon an approaching sleigh in which she recognized the Czar's daughters, Olga and Tatiana, wrapped in furs, their bright faces framed in pointed hoods of dark sealskin.

Katrinka saluted them as she had saluted their father and mother. They smiled in response. But it was evident that they did not recognize either Katrinka or Peter. During their six months in St. Petersburg both children had grown plump and rosy. Katrinka's fur trimmed hood and velvet coat, with its white fox collar and fur lining, were almost as handsome as the hoods and coats of the two Grand Duchesses.

A week later Katrinka began a strange new life. Peter had already been placed in a government school for boys, not far from the home of Madame Morenski, who assured Katrinka that she would keep a watchful eye on him.

The old housekeeper had wept bitterly when she bade the little boy good-by; and later, when the day came for Katrinka to take up her work at the Ballet Institute, the good woman refused to be comforted. She insisted upon going with Katrinka to the very doors of the school, where she clung to her affectionately.

"I shall move at once from Stefan Norvitch's house," she sobbed, "and shall take rooms near your school where I can at least see you every day when you walk with the other pupils, even if I cannot speak with you. And I shall write you many letters."

"And I will write to you, Matuska," cried Katrinka, kissing the good woman, again and again. "You have been like a second mother to Peter and me and when I am through in the school I pray you will come to live with us again."

"You will let me keep your house?"

Katrinka shook her head. "I hope my mother and father will have returned long before then," she said, her lips close to the woman's ear. "Mother will keep the house and you will sit in a big chair with rockers and knit all the day long. We shall be a very happy family."

Once more they kissed each other, then Katrinka disappeared behind the great doors of the ballet school.

Henceforth her days were so full of work that she had little time for mournful thoughts. She slept in a big dormitory with many other little girls. She was awakened at eight o'clock every morning by a deep-voiced bell. She dressed herself in a uniform, consisting of a belted Russian blouse and plaited skirt, thick black stockings and flat-heeled slippers. After she was dressed she reported to a teacher who looked her over to see that her hair had been properly brushed and her hands and face well washed. After this she went to the chapel for prayers, and then breakfast was served on long tables. It was a simple meal consisting merely of tea and bread and butter, with sometimes a little fruit. After breakfast the dancing lessons began. They were given in a big, bright room furnished with benches and many mirrors. These lessons lasted for four hours. The children were drilled in twists and turns, in leaps and pirouettes. Every day they had to stand for many minutes poised on one toe, until sometimes their bodies cried out with pain and weariness.

The dancing lessons were followed by dinner. This was as plain and simple as their clothes. There was porridge, black bread, milk, meat and fruits. No sweets or pastries.

In the afternoon, when often the children's muscles were aching from head to foot from the hard work done in the morning, they attended classes in German, history, music, mathematics and art. These over, they were allowed a half hour for recreation.

But by this time they were too tired for play, so the half hour was usually spent in walking staidly about the streets with their chaperones, for once a child enters the Imperial ballet school she gives up her freedom. She never again appears on the street alone. She belongs to the government. Henceforth her days are devoted to the work of learning how to amuse the Imperial Court. Each group of children has its own police escort, physician and chaperone. When it is necessary for any of the pupils to go to the Imperial Opera House to rehearse, they are driven there and back in Imperial carriages, and although they are but little better off than well cared for slaves, they are happy in their lives and so busy that they do not have time to long for freedom.

One and all they are looking forward to the time when, if they have succeeded in passing their examinations, they will be graduated into the ballet corps as soloists. After becoming a soloist, a dancer receives 8,000 [25] roubles a year. This is paid to her for twenty years, when she is retired from the ballet and is never again allowed to dance. But she receives an income from the government for as long as she lives, which is usually a great many years on account of the excellent training and care she has received in her youth.

A year after Katrinka entered the school, rehearsals were begun for a great spectacle in which all of the children were to take part. It was to be given in the spring, in the park at Tsarskoe Seloe, for the Czar and his family, and was to consist of folk dances, not very different from those which Katrinka had often seen danced on fête days in the village of Vachok.

Katrinka was almost beside herself with delight when she heard of the coming festival, for it meant that she should again see the Czar. Surely this time she would be allowed to speak to him. For had she not become a member of his family of dancers?

She threw herself into her work with all of her strength, and although the line of her cheek thinned and her body became fragile as a snowflake, her dancing seemed never before to have been so joyous or so light. Often in these days the master's eyes followed the child. But Katrinka did not know it. She was so wrapped up in her work that during the practice hours she thought of nothing else.

And then, one wonderful morning, towards the end of the rehearsals, the master took her to one side. "In these little dances which we are practicing," he said, "I am trying to picture the everyday life of the Russian peasant. We have the figures for sowing the seed, for plowing the ground, for harvesting the grain." He paused.

Katrinka raised her eyes questioningly. The master smiled into them.

"I have chosen you, Mademoiselle Katrinka, to dance the part of the good fairy, who flits among the peasants at will, bringing good luck for the sowing and the harvesting, who appears in their midst at the time of marriages and christenings, and who awakens the brown earth to life at Easter."

For a moment Katrinka was too frightened, by this announcement, to thank the master. Her knees trembled.   She felt the color mount in a hot flood to her cheeks.

"Oh, sir," she began.   Then suddenly her mood changed.   Fear melted into joy.   Her eyes were radiant, her face vivid.   She understood the master's announcement.   She was to be the solo dancer at the festival.   It was the greatest honor a little dancing pupil could receive.

"Oh, my master," she exclaimed, "how can I thank you?"   She dropped on her knees and taking his hand kissed his finger tips.   The next moment she sprang to her feet.   "Oh, thank you, thank you!" she cried.

The master patted her head, then motioned her to join the other children.

With steps as gay as a bird's song, as light as thistledown, Katrinka flashed across the floor.   The music struck up, the lesson was continued.

And now came days of the hardest work Katrinka had ever known.   There were times when every muscle in her body felt sore, when her toes were so lame that it seemed as if she could not rise on them at the master's signal. Sometimes an entire morning would be given up to the mastering of a single new step and the master would lose his patience, when, after hours of work, she could not get it.

Her sleep was broken by dreams of the festival. Often she awoke, sobbing, because when the great moment arrived for her to appear before the Czar, she found that she had forgotten the steps she had been practicing.

But during the days these torturing fears did not beset her. Her enthusiasm never flagged. It spread itself to the other children, who threw themselves into their work with new earnestness.

With the approach of spring the difficult exercises seemed to grow easier. The children frolicked through them, led by Katrinka, whose little feet moved so swiftly that it seemed as if the musicians in the orchestra had to play with all their might to keep up with her.

CHAPTER XXVIII

KATRINKA DANCES IN THE FESTIVAL

WHEN the ballet master, and the fifty young girls who were to dance for the Czar, arrived at Tsarskoe Seloe, on the day of the festival, they found half a dozen hay carts waiting at the station. With shouts of delight the children climbed into them, singing as they rattled away towards the palace grounds.

With the exception of Katrinka, all of the girls were dressed in pretty white frocks, their hair tied with big bows of ribbon, their feet encased in heelless dancing shoes. She, alone, wore the dull brown dress, the brown kerchief and the bark sandals of a peasant child. In fact, she was dressed exactly as she had been dressed on the day many weeks ago, when she had first danced for the ballet master.

She looked from one to another of the children, smiling bravely, but there was a lump in her throat. Like every other little girl, she had a fondness for pretty clothes and it grieved her to be the only one among the children dressed in a peasant's skirt and bark sandals.

As she seated herself in the hay cart, one of the older girls, who had not noticed Katrinka before, leaned forward, frowning.

"You are the only one among us in fancy costume," she said. "How did you dare to disobey the master?"

"I did not disobey him," explained Katrinka. "He sent the dress to me."

Two girls sitting nearby overheard the conversation and began to pout.

"Katrinka is the master's pet," said one of them.

The other nodded her head. "Yes, nobody will notice any of the rest of us, to-day, no matter how well we do. It is horrid to be dressed like everybody else."

Katrinka laid her hand soothingly on the girl's arm. "I have been wishing all of the morning that my dress was like the others," she explained. "I am sure everybody will laugh at my awkward shoes and homely skirt."

"Wait and see," said the older girl. "Last year at the children's ballet, a great lady sent a beautiful locket to one of the girls who could dance no better than the rest of us, but who was dressed like a butterfly."

Katrinka laughed, merrily. "But I am not dressed like a beautiful butterfly. I look like a little brown moth that flies around the candle at night. The rest of you are the butterflies."

She clasped her hands against her breast and looked around admiringly. "You are all beautiful," she cried, "like sweet, white blossoms. The Czar and Czarina will be enchanted."

In spite of themselves the other girls smiled pleasantly. Although they sometimes envied Katrinka, they loved her, devotedly. They had found her fair and generous-hearted, always willing to help them in working out difficult steps. She was without envy and and seemed more pleased when others were praised by the master than when she, herself, received a word or smile of commendation.

Presently the hay carts drew up outside the park gates. The children clambered to the ground and went skipping over the grass towards the lake where the gondolas floated. Above the lake, on the terraces, the family and friends of the Czar had gathered to see the festival.

The four little Grand Duchesses were dressed exactly alike in white frocks and blue sashes. Katrinka recognized Olga and Tatiana at once and, as she stood looking up at them, half hoped and half feared that Tatiana would remember her.

Then her eyes fixed themselves upon a great, black man standing behind the Czarina. He was dressed in a uniform of black and gold, and a sword hung at his side. In his arms he held a little boy dressed entirely in white.

Katrinka turned to one of the girls standing nearby.

"Who is the little boy that the black man is holding in his arms?"

"That is Alexis, the Czarevitch," explained the girl. "He was terribly injured a few weeks ago."

"How?" asked Katrinka, wonderingly.

The girl shrugged her shoulders. "Nobody knows. Some say that a sailor attacked him while he was cruising with his parents on their yacht; others say that he had a bad fall, but nobody knows just how it happened."

"Surely nobody would harm a dear little boy like that," began Katrinka.

"Ssh," whispered the girl to whom she was speaking. "There is a Cossack riding up and down. We must not seem to notice that there is anything the matter with the Czarevitch. But look, there is the Czarina! She is lovely, isn't she? She has taken the Czarevitch in her lap."

Katrinka followed the eyes of her friend. The Czarina, dressed in a white gown, had taken her place beside the Grand Duchess Olga. In her lap sat the little Czarevitch. As Katrinka looked at him, the young Grand Duchess Olga covered his feet and legs with a white scarf she was wearing, but not before Katrinka had seen that one of the little boy's knees seemed stiff and rigid. Again she turned questioningly to the older girl. But before she could speak the master's bugle sounded.

"We must form for the dance," cried the older girl.

Katrinka cast one more glance at the group

on the terrace, then joined the other children.

There was a burst of music, and the dancing began. Against the background of great forest trees, the little girls in their light dresses looked like fairies, their movements so light and airy that it seemed almost as if the breezes that stirred the treetops were blowing them about, while in their midst, appearing and disappearing, Katrinka flitted like a butterfly with dull toned wings in a garden of flowers. As she vanished and returned again it seemed to those looking on that her feet needed no resting place for their airy flights. She was here, there, everywhere, and when at last the number ended, seemed to float away into the background.

As she disappeared the music died away. There was a burst of applause from the terraces. It grew louder and louder. The Czarina waved her handkerchief, a man's voice shouted a hurrah.

Almost immediately the band began playing the music for the Czardas.[26]

The master had spent weeks in training Katrinka for this dance, and now as she took her first step he shouted a word of encouragement to her. But she did not hear it, she seemed unconscious of everything but the music. Back and forth she flew, each movement bringing her nearer to the terrace—nearer—nearer —until at last she was only a few yards from the Imperial party and directly below them.

Suddenly the music wound up with a flourish. Katrinka raised her eyes. They met those of the Czarina, who smiled down at the child, wafting her a kiss from her finger tips.

To Katrinka it seemed like an invitation. She sprang forward, then flashed up the steps leading to the top of the terrace, and flung herself, flushed and panting, on her knees at the feet of the Czar.

Instantly there was a great commotion. The Czar sprang to his feet and, taking the Czarevitch from the arms of his wife, whirled around and started towards the palace. The little Grand Duchesses jumped up, took several backward steps, then stopped and stood looking at Katrinka with an expression in which curiosity mingled with fear. The rest of the party, with the exception of the Czarina and an older woman, who, Katrinka afterwards learned was the Czar's mother, scattered in every direction.

For an instant Katrinka knelt on the ground, surprised at the consternation her sudden appearance on the terrace had caused. Then she rose to her feet, looking around wonderingly. Several ladies had dropped their handkerchiefs and parasols in their haste to get away. The Czar had dropped the field-glasses through which he had watched the dancers. They had fallen directly in front of the spot where Katrinka stood. Everybody seemed frightened and upset, excepting the Czarina and the Czar's mother.

"Why has everybody run away?" asked Katrinka. "Is there a fire? I wanted to speak to the Little Father."

Her words were interrupted by a heavy hand on her shoulder. Somebody whirled her around and pushed her roughly towards the steps leading from the terrace.

She pulled back, turning her face in the direction in which the Czar had disappeared, then looking up, met the fierce gaze of one of his Cossacks.

"Oh!" she cried, "please do not take me away. Please do not send me to Siberia. What will Peter do? He is very little!"

The man paid no attention to her words. He dragged her down the steps and lifted her to one of the park benches. In the meantime several other guards had emerged from the shrubbery about the lake and now came rushing up. In their midst was the ballet master, gesticulating wildly and trying to explain that Katrinka meant no harm.

But the Cossacks would not believe him. They searched Katrinka from head to foot, treating her so roughly that bruises appeared on her arms and shoulders. But she did not cry out nor make a struggle to free herself, although her face was white and her eyes blazed. She realized that she was suspected of being in a plot to harm the Czar or the little Czarevitch and that resistance would be useless.

It was not until they had pulled off her bark sandals and the strappings about her legs that the Cossacks, with an angry shove, turned her over to the ballet master, who stood nearby, waving his arms and talking very fast.

"She is a mere baby," he cried. "She wanted to kiss His Majesty's hand. I beseech you to let the child go. She will be unfit for dancing for weeks to come after your harsh treatment."

He wrung his hands distractedly. The Cossacks shrugged their shoulders.

"Take the child from the park, immediately," they commanded.

Nervous and frowning, the master took Katrinka by the hand and, followed by one of the guards, went with her to the park gates, where the hay carts were waiting to take the children away.

That evening in St. Petersburg the story was told of how a little girl had tried to destroy the Czar and his family during the children's festival. Of course, there was no truth in the tale, but it caused the ballet master a great deal of annoyance and, for some time afterwards, secret officers lurked about in the neighborhood of the school watching the goings and comings of the children.

CHAPTER XXIX

KATRINKA ENTERS THE IMPERIAL BALLET

NEARLY three years after the children's festival in the park at Tsarskoe Seloe, where Katrinka had tried vainly to speak to the Czar, the dancing master came to her at the close of the afternoon lesson and spread before her an official-looking paper. It was covered with seals and signatures. Katrinka looked at it, then turned to the master.

"What is it?" she asked,

"It is your contract with the Czar."

"I do not understand," said Katrinka.

"I have arranged for your appearance at the Imperial Theater. In this contract you promise to dance three evenings a week. In return you will receive eight thousand roubles a year. In the contract you will agree that you will not dance outside of St. Petersburg without permission from the Czar, otherwise you will forfeit your life pension which begins when you are thirty-six. Next week you will leave the school and go with your chaperone to live in a house near the theater."

"And Peter—my little brother—" began Katrinka.

"He will continue in school. But you may see him as often as you wish."

Katrinka clasped her hands. "Oh, how good everybody is to us," she cried. Then her face fell.

"I wish father knew that Peter was going to school. He told me to take the tin box and go to Stefan Norvitch in St. Petersburg and to ask him to send Peter to school. An officer carried away the tin box, and the morning after we found Stefan Norvitch he was shot by the Cossacks. Please tell me why people are so kind to me and so cruel to people who are so very good, like Stefan Norvitch and my father and mother."

"They are good to you, child, because you have a great gift. In Russia the path is made easy for all artists. From now on, you will be deprived of nothing that is within reason. You are setting out upon a great career. I shall continue to instruct you. But when the time comes when you no longer require the services of a master, remember to keep your work poetic and noble. Now sign your name to this paper. It is the Czar's contract with you. He engages you to dance for twenty seasons in the Imperial ballet."

The master held out a pen. Katrinka hesitated. "But he has not seen me dance since the children's festival, when he ran away from me."

A smile twisted the master's mouth.

"But he has heard of you. He sees very few of the artists whom he engages. He does not even know that Katrinka Petrovna is the young girl who caused so much commotion in the park at Tsarskoe Seloe."

Katrinka's heart sank. "Then, perhaps, he will never see me dance. I can never tell him my story after all."

"You are impatient, child. All that you wish will come in good time."

He gave Katrinka the pen and pointed to a line at the foot of the document. "Write your name there."

Very carefully Katrinka penned her name beneath that of the Czar. When she had finished, the master folded the paper and put it into his pocket.

"We shall begin rehearsing at the Imperial theater to-morrow. This afternoon Madame Morenski will call for you and for the woman who has taken care of you so long. A governess has been engaged to teach you French and music. You will in future be a protégée of the Emperor and Empress of Russia. Your life will be ordered very much like that of a child of noble birth."

Half an hour later the news of Katrinka's good fortune had been spread throughout the school, and by the time she was ready to start for home, she was surrounded by girls eager to question her and to wish her luck. Several of the older girls in the school had also signed contracts. Others had been disappointed. Some of these would be allowed to continue at the school for another year; but those who failed utterly would be compelled to give up the work.

Now began for Katrinka a very wonderful time. She moved from the ballet school to some bright rooms overlooking a park. They were very nicely furnished, and heated with a porcelain stove set in the wall so that it projected into the parlor on one side and into Katrinka's bedroom on the other. The house had double windows, and in each window was a single pane of glass that could be opened to let in the air.

The chaperone who had watched over Katrinka at the ballet school came to live with her, and so also did Stefan Norvitch's housekeeper, as happy as a child that she was again under the same roof with Katrinka.

Every day Katrinka had lessons with the dancing masters, but they were given in the Imperial theater now and the steps that it had once seemed impossible to master were no longer difficult. They seemed like simple words used to express the meaning of the music to which she danced.

Early in January the opening ball of the season in St. Petersburg was given at the Winter Palace, and the lovely young Madame Morenski who, Katrinka had learned at the ballet school, was a great favorite in society, received an invitation. The following day she called at the theater where Katrinka was rehearsing.

"I am going home with you this afternoon," she said, as Katrinka stepped into her low sledge, driven by a coachman wearing a coat so wadded and padded to keep out the cold that he looked curiously like a big feather pillow. "We will have tea together and make plans for the ball at the Winter Palace. I have decided to take you to see it. The Grand Duchess Olga will be present. It will be her first great ball."

"Will the Grand Duchess Tatiana be there too?" asked Katrinka, her eyes sparkling at the promised gayety.

"No, she is not yet sixteen. Her parents think her too young to attend court balls."

"I am not sixteen, either," said Katrinka, fearful that when she confessed her age Madame Morenski would withdraw her invitation. "I am only fifteen."

"You are not a Czar's daughter," laughed Madame Morenski. "Besides, you are merely going to look on. I thought it would interest you. The Emperor and Empress will open the Polonaise."

"Will they dance the Komarinskaia?" [27]

Madame Morenski laughed softly. "No,

indeed, Katrinka. The balls at the Winter Palace are very ceremonious affairs, at which a great many people merely promenade about the ballroom or look on from the balconies. The dances are slow and stately. You will see nothing so difficult as the Komarinskaia. There will be the Polonaise [28] and a few simple waltzes. That is all. But the music and the decorations of the room are wonderful. If you go, even to look on, you ought to have a new frock—something simple, of course—and —I wonder what color would best suit you!"

"Mother used to like to see me in white on gala days," said Katrinka, simply.

"Then white you shall wear," said Madame Morenski. "We will order the dress to-morrow, for the ball is less than a week away."

CHAPTER XXX

KATRINKA ATTENDS A BALL AT THE WINTER PALACE

THE night of the great ball was so cold that huge bonfires were lighted in the squares adjoining the Winter Palace. About them were gathered the coachmen and sledge drivers wrapped in their wadded coats, over which many of them wore capes of fur with high fur collars. Huge fur caps were pulled over their foreheads and ears; yet in spite of their heavy clothing and the blazing bonfires, they found it necessary to stamp their feet and slap their hands constantly against their chests to keep warm.

Madame Morenski had brought an extra fur robe in which she wrapped Katrinka before setting out, for when it was learned at the Imperial theater that she intended taking the child to the ball at the Winter Palace, the doctor, who is employed by the Czar and Czarina to look after the health of the young dancers at the theater, scolded her roundly. He warned her that she would be held responsible if Katrinka contracted a cold. Madame Morenski laughed at his fears and assured him that Katrinka would be well protected.

But in spite of Madame Morenski's precautions, the curls about Katrinka's forehead, her brows and lashes were white with frost when the sleigh drew up in front of the Palace, and her eyelids felt stiff from the cold. As she stepped from the sleigh, she paused for a moment to look at the great bonfires in the square. Besides the drivers in their wadded coats, hundreds of beggars had gathered about them and stood holding their hands to the blaze, while the cruel winds whipped their clothing about their shivering bodies.

A great throb of pity seemed to choke Katrinka for a moment; then she turned and followed Madame Morenski into the Winter Palace.

A few minutes later she stood on the threshold of the ballroom, her lips parted, her eyes wide with wonder. The great, stately room was lighted with thousands of wax candles, and moving about on its polished floor were throngs of people, the women in trailing gowns, their throats and hair glittering with jewels. All about the walls were stationed guards in brilliant uniforms and, at the end of the room, flanked by Cossacks, stood the Czar. Beside him was the Czarina in a gown of white satin with an enormous train of white velvet.

"The Polonaise is beginning," murmured Madame Morenski. "The Emperor and Empress are leading it."

As she spoke, Katrinka saw the Czar take the hand of the Czarina and holding it very high, come slowly towards them. Behind him came other couples, the men in uniform, the women wearing gowns with long trains spread over the floor behind them. It was a beautiful sight, and Katrinka watched it with shining eyes. When at last the Czar and Czarina had made the complete circle of the great ballroom, they walked slowly back to the middle of the floor, where the Empress made a deep curtsey and backed towards the side of the room. The Emperor immediately escorted another woman to the middle of the floor, holding her hand high and walking with her slowly about the room as he had done before. Katrinka noticed that other men, instead of leaving their partners in the middle of the floor, escorted them back to their seats. She looked up at Madame Morenski questioningly.

"Why did the Czar leave the Czarina to find a seat for herself," she asked, "when all of the other gentlemen bow to their partners after showing them a nice place to sit down?"

Madame Morenski laughed. "You pretend to be a Russian child, Katrinka, and yet you do not know that the Emperor is higher and more important than any other person in all the empire. The Empress must curtsey to him, of course, and get back to her seat as well as she can alone. I assure you it is a difficult feat when one has such a heavy train as hers to manage. But she did it nicely."

"Will the Emperor walk with you?" asked Katrinka, thinking that her friend looked prettier than any of the other women she had yet seen in the ballroom.

"No, indeed. I doubt if he will remember me. I am a very insignificant person compared with most of the ladies here. Besides, he must dance with the wives of all the foreign ambassadors to-night. By the time he has led each one of them out, it will be morning. But see, the Empress is about to dance. She has chosen a handsome young man for her partner."

Katrinka looked towards the Empress, then turned towards Madame Morenski. The ball-room floor had been cleared as if by magic of everybody excepting the Empress and a young man in uniform.

"The music is playing," said Katrinka. "Why is nobody excepting the Czarina and the young man dancing?"

"When the Empress of Russia chooses a partner for the waltz or mazurka, all other dancers must at once stop in order that the floor may be clear for her," explained Madame Morenski. "How flushed her cheeks are. She is evidently embarrassed to have so many people staring at her. She is as shy as any schoolgirl. I am surprised that she asked the young man to dance."

As Madame Morenski finished speaking, the

Empress returned to her place at the end of
the room and immediately the floor refilled
with dancers.

A young man in a coat blazing with medals
came up and asked Madame Morenski to
dance. She refused him with an enchanting
smile.

"I am not dancing to-night," she said. "I
came in order that my little friend, Katrinka
Petrovna, could see the opening ball of the St.
Petersburg season. But pray tell me the name
of the young man with whom the Empress
danced a moment since. He is a stranger to
me."

"Have you not heard the latest court gos-
sip? The young man is Prince Charles, the
oldest son of the Crown Prince of Roumania.
It is said that the Grand Duchess Olga is engaged to him."

Madame Morenski laughed. "She has been
reported engaged to no less than a dozen
princes."

"And she is not yet eighteen," added the
young officer. "But see, she is dancing with
the young man."

Katrinka's eyes flashed from one dancing

couple to another, finally discovering the Grand
Duchess Olga and the young prince. They
had just stopped dancing and were walking
slowly towards a great, arched doorway beyond which Katrinka could see a forest of
enormous palms.

"The Grand Duchess Olga and Prince
Charles are going into the supper-room," said
Madame Morenski. "Let us follow them.
There will be a crush about the tables pres-
ently."

The young officer offered an arm to both
Madame Morenski and Katrinka, and together
the three made their way to the doorway
through which the Grand Duchess Olga had
disappeared. On the threshold of the room,
Katrinka paused. "Is it fairyland come
true?" she gasped, looking about delightedly.

The great room had been transformed to
look like a garden in midsummer. There were
groups of flowering lilacs, laburnums and
syringas growing in beds that blazed with
tulips, daffodils and crocuses. Sandy paths
led to enormous palms. The walls of the room
were concealed by arbors covered with honey-
suckle and climbing roses.

For several seconds Katrinka gazed at the scene, enraptured. Had some fairy touched the world with a magic wand and changed winter into summer in an hour, she asked herself.

The young officer, catching the surprised look in her wide eyes, laughed. "It is a wonderful scene," he said. "These flowering shrubs were brought up yesterday from the greenhouses at Tsarskoe Seloe. The gardeners have been forcing them for weeks in order to have them in bloom for to-night. But behold the tables! There are five thousand people here to-night. After supper we will go to the kitchen and watch the bargaining."

This time it was Madame Morenski's turn to look surprised.

"Watch the bargaining?" she asked. "What do you mean?"

"Have you never heard of the remnant-sale that follows a ball at the Winter Palace?" asked the young officer as they seated themselves at one of the little tables. "What did you suppose became of the left-over delicacies?"

"I supposed they were given to the poor, or sent to the hospitals."

The young officer laughed again. "No, indeed. I will show you what becomes of the viands after the supper is over. The Emperor pays the *chef* so much a plate for serving the five thousand guests. The *chef* orders what he pleases, receives the money from the Emperor and then makes a comfortable little fortune from the left-overs."

The supper was elaborate, but Katrinka hardly realized what she ate, so interested was she in watching the throngs who strolled about under the trees, or formed merry parties around the tables.

Immediately after supper the young officer led the way to the kitchen, where Counts, Barons, hotel proprietors and even Grand Dukes were bargaining with the *chef* for the remains of the feast. It was very amusing to watch these men as they bid excitedly for the lobster mayonnaise, the ices, the cakes and the candied fruits.

When at last Madame Morenski turned away from the interesting scene, Katrinka

sighed, looking back many times as they passed
down the stairs and through the lines of sentries that guarded the entrance. As she stood
for a moment under the frosty, starlit sky, she
saw that the bonfires surrounding the Winter
Palace still burned. About them were gathered the half-frozen coachmen in their wadded
caftans [29] and the beggars in their rags.

"Oh!" cried Katrinka, grasping the arm of
Madame Morenski, "I had forgotten the cold.
Inside the palace there are flowers, although
it is mid-winter. There is so much food that
the people cannot eat it. It is so warm that
I felt beads of moisture on my forehead; and
yet, out here there are men and women who
are freezing—and, oh! perhaps they are
hungry."

"Yes, Katrinka," replied Madame Morenski
sadly, "it is because of these contrasts between
wealth and poverty that half the people in Russia are revolutionists.[30] But get into the
sledge at once, you will take cold standing
here."

Katrinka climbed into the sledge, the driver
cracked his whip and the horses sprang forward. Presently, they had left the Winter

Palace far behind them. Only the sleigh-bells and the sound of the horses' hoofs broke the silence. Madame Morenski leaned forward and looked down into Katrinka's face. Katrinka smiled up at her wistfully.

"I am thinking," she said, "of Ivan Drovski and his family in the village of Vachok. There are six children, and in the winter they all sleep on top of the stove with Mother Drovski. There are only two rooms in the izba, and after the snow comes, Ivan must give one of these to the cow and the chickens and the little pigs, to keep them from freezing."

Madame Morenski slipped her arm around Katrinka. "There are many, many families in Russia who live like that, little Katrinka," she said. "My dear young brother used to spend much time among them, showing them how to build better houses and teaching the children to read and write. Alas! five years ago he was sent to Siberia. He has been pardoned, but he is no longer allowed to carry on his work."

As Madame Morenski finished speaking, the horses drew up beside the curb. Katrinka pushed back the robe and jumped to the ground. Madame Morenski stretched out her hand, and drawing the child to her, kissed her lightly on the forehead.

"Good-night, Katrinka," she said. "I will see you again soon."

She smiled brightly. As the horses dashed away, Katrinka brushed her hand across her eyes. For a moment she had fancied that it was the face of the young man who had come to the church on Easter morning, with the letter from her parents, that she had seen smiling down upon her from Madame Morenski's fur-lined hood.

Later, as she sat brushing and braiding her hair before her little dressing-table, she thought again of the gaunt young man with the hollow eyes but the sunny smile, who had come to the village of Vachok on Easter morning.

"Shall I ever see him again?" she asked herself as she slipped into bed. The recollection of his face had banished the memory of the gay ball at the Winter Palace, and of the square with its blazing bonfires and its shivering men and women.

CHAPTER XXXI

IT was the night of Katrinka's first appearance in the Imperial Ballet. The great theater was filled to overflowing.

Madame Morenski, in a gown of gold colored satin, occupied a seat near the stage. It had come down to her from a great grandfather and she owned it just as she owned the house in which she lived. On all sides of her were gathered the nobles and great ladies of Russia, all of them occupying seats which had descended to them from their forefathers. For in the great opera house in St. Petersburg, every seat on the main floor is hereditary, it cannot be bought or sold. When a stranger wishes to attend a performance he cannot sit on the main floor unless he is the guest of somebody owning a seat. If he has no friends who are seat-owners he must buy a place in the gallery or balcony.

As Madame Morenski swept down the aisle of the opera house many faces were turned towards her and there immediately arose the sound of subdued voices, for it was well known in St. Petersburg that it was she who had discovered the young girl who was appearing that night for the first time in the Imperial Ballet and who, it was said, would soon be the greatest dancer in Russia.

With Madame Morenski, occupying the seat that belonged to her brother, was a little boy with dark eyes and thick hair. He climbed into his place, then turned and looked around. His skin was brown, his cheeks full and very red. Some of the people sitting near began to whisper.

"The little boy is the brother of Mademoiselle Petrovna," said one.

"Yes. I understand they were peasant children and very poor when Madame Morenski found them."

"It is rumored that their parents are in Siberia."

The little boy, hearing the buzz of voices

all about him, looked up questioningly into the face of Madame Morenski.

"Will Katrinka be afraid?" he asked.

"No, Peter, she will think only of her dancing," replied Madame Morenski, reassuringly. But there was a tremor in her voice, and in her long gloves her fingers felt like ice.

The little boy settled down beside her, then suddenly leaned forward, his sharp eyes on a box at the right of the stage. Four people had just entered it. They were the Czar and Czarina of Russia and their two oldest daughters, the Grand Duchesses, Olga and Tatiana.

Madame Morenski laid her arm across her small companion's shoulders.

"That is the Czar, Nicholas II," she began. "He has come to see Katrinka dance. You have not forgotten the Grand Duchess Tatiana?"

A little bell tinkled somewhere. A burst of music drowned Peter's reply. The curtain went up. The performance began.

The scene on the stage was like fairyland. There were trees and flowers and dozens of dainty young dancers in exquisite colors. Even Madame Morenski had never seen anything more beautiful, and little Peter was carried away with it. He clapped his hands delightedly and then, suddenly remembering his sister, looked up at Madame Morenski with troubled eyes.

"Where is Katrinka?" he asked, aloud.

"Ssh! She will come presently. But you must talk in whispers or you will disturb others."

As Madame Morenski finished speaking, a slender sprite appeared at the back of the stage, hovered there for a moment, and then floated forward with such airy grace and lightness that the whole audience rose to give her welcome.

"Katrinka, Katrinka!" Little Peter's voice rang out in an appeal for recognition. But for once Katrinka did not hear it. She was unconscious of her surroundings, lost in the joy of movement. She danced with the lightness of the wind, the gayety of rippling waters. St. Petersburg had never before seen such tender, joyous, dainty movement. It was as if the spirit of childhood had been captured and then set free on the stage of the gray old opera house,—the spirit of childhood, gay, witching, light, and yet unutterably sad.   It brought a lump into the throat of every one of the onlookers and, when at last, Katrinka, as if blown like a rose petal to the back of the stage, where she remained poised on her toes for a moment, disappeared, a sigh that was like a sob ran over the house.   It was followed by a great burst of applause, and Madame Morenski, looking around, felt suddenly relieved.   Katrinka had danced her way straight into the hearts of the people.   They loved her.

The house rocked with the bravos which followed the dropping of the curtain.   For fully ten minutes they kept up.   The Czar and his family joined in them, but little Katrinka did not reappear.   For in Russia the members of the Czar's ballet are not allowed to respond to applause by so much as a smile or a sidelong glance of gratitude.

Katrinka, in her dressing room, heard the shouts and the handclapping that rocked the house, and wished that she could go before the curtain and blow a kiss to the audience.

"Oh, I hope they know how I love them all,"

she whispered to herself. "And how much I thank them for being so very, very good to me."

Then a shadow crossed her forehead. She was thinking of the Czar in his box near the stage. Would the time ever come when she would be allowed to speak to him? To tell him her story?

A loud rap on her door interrupted her thoughts. She opened it to face a little page who said that her carriage was waiting outside. Katrinka slipped into the fur-lined coat, which her chaperone held. Then, together, the two left the opera house.

The streets outside were lined with people. As Katrinka appeared they surged forward. The police tried vainly to hold them back. But it was no use. They unhitched the horses from Katrinka's carriage. She stepped into it and it rolled away, drawn by dozens of human hands.

As she passed through the cheering throngs Katrinka leaned forward, smiling and bowing from right to left. Then, gradually, as her excitement died away, her heart grew heavy.

It was not for applause that she had danced. It was to please the Little Father, to reach his heart, so that one day he would let her come before him and on her knees implore him to hear her story.

When at last Katrinka reached home and went to her room at the top of the house, she found a letter propped against the mirror of her dressing table. It was sealed with a golden eagle.

The blood leaped to her cheeks. With trembling fingers she picked up the envelope, pressed it to her lips, then broke the seal. A moment later she cried out in delight, for the letter enclosed was from the Czar of all the Russias. He summoned her to appear on the following Saturday afternoon at his private theater in Tsarskoe Seloe.

Katrinka's eyes burned with excitement as she sat down at her little desk to pen a reply. At last her prayers were to be answered. She was to have an audience with the Czar. The long, hard years of work in the Imperial Ballet school were to be rewarded. She opened her portfolio and took from it a sheet of paper.

On it she longed to pour out her heart, to write her whole story, to pray for the return of her parents.

Instead, she began to write slowly and very carefully, for one cannot write as one will to the Czar of all the Russias. Certain laws must be obeyed when addressing him. Katrinka knew them well, and instead of the letter which her heart urged her to write she penned a stiff and formal note.

"His Majesty, Czar Nicholas II,
          "The Winter Palace, St. Petersburg.
"Your Imperial Highness:
     "It gives me great pleasure to accept the summons of Your Majesty to dance before you on Saturday afternoon at two o'clock in the Palace at Tsarskoe Seloe.

     "If it is not too presuming I humbly pray that at the close of the performance Your Majesty will grant me a short interview.

     "Faithfully the servant of Your Imperial Highness,

                    "Katrinka Petrovna."

After dispatching the note Katrinka ate a light supper, then went to bed. But she could not sleep. She lay awake until almost morning, planning what she should say to the Little Father when the wonderful day arrived.

During the remainder of that week she seemed to move in a dream, from which she awakened only when the hour came for her to appear in the ballet. She lost her appetite, and Stefan Norvitch's housekeeper worried and scolded as one after another of the dainty dishes she prepared was left untasted.

"You do not eat enough to keep a bird alive," she grumbled. "I shall ask your chaperone to report you to the ballet master. You are starving yourself to death."

In reply Katrinka laughed and gave the woman an affectionate hug.

"You shall have no cause to complain after Saturday, Matushka. I shall eat so much that my cheeks will look like puff balls, and my hands will be as dimpled as little Peter's." Then she breathed a great sigh. "Oh, will Saturday never come?" she murmured, shaking her head.

It did at last and Katrinka, in company with her master and her chaperone, started for Tsarskoe Seloe. They arrived in good time

and at the appointed hour Katrinka appeared
on the stage of the Czar's private theater.

The audience that had gathered to see her
was small, made up of the relatives and most
intimate friends of the Czar and his family.
The little Czarevitch sat in a box between his
father and mother, looking rosier and plumper
that when Katrinka had last seen him. Behind him sat Tatiana, grown tall and beautiful, although her eyes still had the merry
twinkle that Katrinka remembered.

Olga, Marie and Anastasia were also there
and they gave the little dancer, who had cap-
tivated St. Petersburg a few evenings before,
a warm welcome.

As when Katrinka had appeared in the
Opera House, her dancing was like a fairy
tale. At the end of it, before the curtain
dropped, the Czarina leaned forward and taking a great bunch of violets from her corsage,
threw it at Katrinka's feet. In her dressing
room Katrinka kissed the flowers. Then, with
trembling fingers she helped her attendant un-
fasten her dancing costume, which she changed
for the simple dress of blue flannel, with its

loosely belted Russian blouse, that she had worn as a pupil in the Ballet Institute.

She had barely finished knotting her tie when a lad in a Cossack's uniform announced that their Imperial Highnesses would see Mademoiselle Petrovna.

Katrinka followed the messenger through the dusky corridors of the theater, through several stately rooms and up a broad flight of stairs, at the top of which two footmen in livery stood on guard.

"Mademoiselle Petrovna," murmured the Cossack to the first of these footmen. Then bowed, turned on his heel, and went down the stairs.

"Mademoiselle Petrovna," murmured the first footman without turning his head.

"Mademoiselle Petrovna," repeated the second footman, drawing aside a heavy velvet curtain and displaying a spacious room decorated in white and lilac color.

Katrinka started forward, then paused. Her knees were trembling, her lips dry and parched. She was frightened by the severe and haughty expressions on the faces of the guards. The things she had planned to say and do were forgotten. She wished that she had not asked to see the Czar but had written her story to him when she had accepted his summons to the palace. If a single Cossack and two young footmen could so frighten her, what would happen when she faced the Czar himself?

"Madamoiselle Petrovna," repeated the guard. He still held back the curtain.

Katrinka summoned all of her courage. She took a step forward. Her lips were compressed, her icy fingers clasped. The curtain dropped behind her. She raised her eyes and found herself gazing into the gentle face of the Czarina. Beside her stood the Czar, his lips parted in a smile. The Czarina was holding out her hand.

Katrinka's fear dropped from her like a cloak. She looked from one kind face to the other; then, taking the Czarina's outstretched hand, kissed its fingers with childish impulsiveness.

"Your Majesties," she began, and curtsied.

"You wished to see me," said the Czar, genially, as if to reassure her.

"Oh, yes, Your Majesty. I have tried many times to see you. I have much to tell you. Now that I am here you will listen to my story, will you not?"

The Czar's face clouded. "Certainly, my child," he replied and led the way to a group of chairs near the window. "It seems that everybody in Russia has a story, even the children."

He seated himself. The Czarina took a place beside him. Katrinka sank on a footstool at their feet.

"Your dancing has interested us," said the Czarina, kindly. "You are young to have graduated into the ballet."

"I am fifteen, Your Majesty," said Katrinka, trying vainly to keep her voice from trembling. "And I have danced all of my life. When I was a very small child and lived in the village of Vachok with my father and mother, I danced to the folk songs."

The Czarina sighed. "And your father and mother are no longer living," she said.

"Oh, yes," cried Katrinka. "They are living, Your Majesty, but they—"

"I understood that you were an orphan."

interrupted the Czar. "A protégée of Madame Morenski."

"Madame Morenski has been very kind to me. It was she who first took me to the ballet school. But, Your Majesties, my father and mother are living. It is on their account that I wished to see you. My father's name is Peter Petrovski. We lived in the village of Vachok, at the end of the street, in the large house. It had two rooms and a store room and we had a stable to shelter our cow and hens. In the winter the village children used to come to our house to learn reading and writing, and sometimes in the evenings father held meetings in the big room where the loom stood. But one night the Cossacks came and carried him and mother away, and Peter and I were left alone. Oh, Your Majesties, it was very cruel, for father loved you, and your pictures hung beside the sacred images above the table. Peter and I have been very lonely ever since, and sometimes we have been hungry, and oh, we have missed our father and mother so very, very much. They were true and faithful to Your Majesties, always, and they taught Peter and me to love you dearly. And so I have come to beseech you to restore them to us. If they were bad I should not ask you to bring them back, but they were good and loyal subjects. You may send your officers to the village of Vachok and ask about them. I am sure that everybody will tell you that my father loved his Czar. He taught us to call you the Little Father and—"

"What was your father's name, Mademoiselle?" The Czar's voice sounded stern. The lines in his face had hardened. Katrinka glanced appealingly at the Czarina. Her face had clouded but her eyes were full of sympathy.

"My father's name is Peter Petrovski," repeated Katrinka.

"How old were you when he was taken away?" asked the Czarina, leaning forward.

"I was ten years old."

"And how long after that did you come to St. Petersburg?" There was a kind note in the Czar's voice. Katrinka heard it and her courage returned.

"In the spring after father and mother were taken away. We took our samovar to the bazaar and sold it. For we were starving.

Her Highness, the Grand Duchess Tatiana, picked us up on the road and drove us a part of the way. I am sure she will remember how she asked us to get into her carriage and then drove us to the village of Tosna, where we stayed for three days. And perhaps Your Majesties will remember how at The Parade of Girls on the Monday after Pentecost, a little peasant girl danced at the foot of the terrace. You sent money to her."

"Are you the peasant child who danced that day?" exclaimed the Czar, smiling again. "I remember it well. We have often spoken of you and wondered what had become of you." He rose and Katrinka knew that she was dismissed.

"And my father and mother—" she began, desperately.

"I shall have their case investigated, Mademoiselle."

The stern note had returned to the Czar's voice.

"I thank Your Majesty and, ah, if you will only restore our father and mother to Peter and me, our blessings will follow you all of your life."

Katrinka made a deep curtsey. She would have liked to kiss the Czar's fingers but his hands were clasped behind him. She backed slowly towards the door where she made a second curtsey. As she rose from it her eyes met those of the Czar. He smiled at her with wonderful kindness. Katrinka smiled back and as the guard, who was waiting outside the room, held back the curtain, she saluted prettily, then disappeared.

CHAPTER XXXII

HER HEART'S DESIRE

MADAME MORENSKI stood in front of
the porcelain stove in her drawing room,
waiting for the sledge which was to take her to
a reception at the Winter Palace.

The ballet season was drawing to a close
and Madame Morenski was thinking of little
Katrinka Petrovna and of her wonderful success as a dancer. Katrinka's picture smiled
from shop windows and her name was known
to every child and grown-up person in St.
Petersburg. Yet Katrinka's head had not
been turned. She seemed the same simple,
sweet natured little girl that Madame Morenski
had first seen dancing to the playing of the old
musician in the house of Stefan Norvitch.
Her eyes still had their wistful expression, her
lips a pathetic droop.

Madame Morenski's thoughts were interrupted by the ringing of a bell. Her sledge

must have arrived. She picked up her long, fur-lined coat, then turned as the door was flung suddenly open.

"Sister!" A tall young man in a sheepskin coat, such as peasants wear, sprang into the room.

"Brother!" Madame Morenski threw her arms impulsively about the young man's neck. "I am so very glad to see you," she cried. "But what brings you to St. Petersburg without warning?"

"I have come to meet friends from the village of Vachok," replied her brother, kissing her heartily. "They are in great trouble. They are seeking—"

His words were interrupted by the appearance of a man in livery. "Your sledge is waiting, Madame," announced the newcomer.

"Do not let me detain you," said Madame Morenski's brother, picking up the fur-lined coat that had fallen to the floor. "I stopped for a moment only. I am looking for two children who disappeared some years ago from the village of Vachok. It is believed that—"

"You are looking for some children who disappeared from the village of Vachok? How long ago?" Madame Morenski's soft eyes blazed with excitement.

"Five years."

Madame Morenski grasped her brother's arm. "What were their names?"

"Petrovski."

The light faded from Madame Morenski's eyes. "I had hoped that it was Petrovna." She paused, then clasped her hands delightedly. "Petrovna and Petrovski! There is but very little difference between the names. What were the first names of these children?"

"Katrinka and Peter. Their parents are beside themselves with grief. They were torn from their little ones five years ago and sent to Siberia. They arrived there just before the end of my own exile. Last week they were pardoned by the Czar. They returned home only to learn that their children had disappeared. They came to St. Petersburg, hoping to find the little ones at the house of Stefan Norvitch. But, alas, Stefan Norvitch is dead. Strangers live in his house—"

"Seek no farther," cried Madame Morenski. "All St. Petersburg knows the whereabouts of Katrinka Petrovna, or Petrovski, as you call her. She is the dancer whose face smiles from the window of every shop in the city—"

"I do not understand," interrupted the young man.

"Have you not heard of Mademoiselle Petrovna?"

"Yes. But what has she to do with these children, Katrinka and Peter Petrovski—"

"Mademoiselle Petrovna is Katrinka Petrovski. Come. I will take you to her at once."

Her brother looked at Madame Morenski, dazedly, shaking his head as if he doubted her sanity.

"These children whom I seek are peasant children," he began.

Madame Morenski laughed softly and slipped her arms into her coat.

"Come with me. I will soon convince you that the little peasant girl for whom you are looking is no other than the wonderful dancer, Mademoiselle Katrinka Petrovna."

"It is impossible," insisted her brother, as he opened the door. "Peter Petrovski would have recognized his own child if, as you say, her pictures are everywhere."

"Ah, but she has changed. She has grown marvelously beautiful, and, besides, her parents think of her as a little girl in a brown peasant's dress and bark sandals, with a kerchief tied about her ears. They have not thought to look for a resemblance between their daughter and Mademoiselle Petrovna, dressed like a butterfly, and the most wonderful dancer in Russia."

Madame Morenski stepped into the sleigh, then gave the driver the number of Katrinka's house. Still but half convinced, her brother joined her. The driver flourished his whip. The horses tossed their heads, and with a great jangling of bells, leaped forward.

Five minutes later Madame Morenski was rapping at Katrinka's door. It was opened by Peter, who was spending the day with his sister. Near the window Katrinka sat, sewing. She sprang to her feet as Madame Morenski entered, holding out her hand and smiling a welcome.

"I have a wonderful surprise for you," cried Madame Morenski, waving away the outstretched hand and running to a closet, from which she took Peter's coat. "Put on your bonnet and some warm wraps, at once, Katrinka," she went on excitedly, as she buttoned Peter into his overcoat. "My brother is waiting outside in the sledge. He has great news."

Katrinka asked no questions. She tied her fur-lined hood under her chin, slipped into her coat and, taking Peter by the hand, ran down the stairs after Madame Morenski, whose feet seemed suddenly winged.

"This is my brother, Aleck—" began Madame Morenski, but before she could finish the introduction Katrinka was holding out her hands.

"Oh, I have wondered if I should ever see you again," she cried, looking into the eyes of Madame Morenski's brother. "Have you come once more with word from our parents?" She turned to Madame Morenski. *"He—he* is the young man who came to the church on Easter morning with word from father and mother." Again she whirled around, her eager gaze on the young man's face. "I can read in your eyes that you have seen father and mother. Oh, tell me, what is the message you bring?"

"They are here—in St. Petersburg. They are looking for you and Peter."

Katrinka jumped into the sleigh, kissed the young man on the cheek, as she had done on Easter morning, then turned to Madame Morenski. "Oh, let us make haste—let us make haste," she cried. "I will take Peter in my lap. It seems as if I could not wait to see them. Tell me, quickly, are they well?"

The driver raised his whip and the horses plunged forward.

"Very well, but very unhappy because they could not find you." The young man looked into Katrinka's flushed face. In his eyes there was an expression of tenderness. Seeing it, Katrinka blushed, and remembering her impulsive kiss, shrank from him, shyly.

In front of a tall red brick house, not far from the Winter Palace, the horses were drawn up. Madame Morenski's brother sprang from the sledge and held out his arms for Peter. Katrinka jumped lightly to the ground without his assistance and, running up the steps, pulled at the old fashioned door bell.

A moment later the door of the house swung in. Then, before anybody had time to speak, there was the sound of hurrying footsteps at the head of the stairs. The next moment Katrinka was folded in her mother's arms and Peter was shouting hurrahs from his father's shoulder.

Tears rose to Madame Morenski's eyes. She laid her hand on her brother's arm. Softly they withdrew, leaving the reunited family together.

NOTES

No. 1. Katrinka:—Affectionate diminutive of *Eka-terina* (Katharine).

No. 2. Mamusia:—Little Mother.

No. 3. Samovar:—The large copper vessel heated by charcoal, in which the Russians boil water for tea.

No. 4. Matuska:—Childish name for Mother. Matusia and Matushka are variations of this name.

No. 5. The Little Man Behind the Chimney:—Among the Russian peasants a little man is supposed to live behind the chimneys. For his comfort the fire in the stove is always kept burning, both winter and summer.

No. 6. Cossacks:—This word came from the Tartar word, kazak, meaning robber. The original Cossacks were a mixed race of Russians, Poles, Tartars, and other wild adventurers. They lived in the territory south of Russia and Poland, and finally all of them became a part of the Russian Empire. They are handsome, daring, and have no fear of death. They are always ready to fight, and the Czar of Russia considers them the most valuable of all his troops. The Czar's bodyguard is made up of Cossacks who wear the original savage dress of their tribe, consisting of a high fur hat, a red or brown coat with sash, and a cartridge belt across the chest.

No. 7. Basket:—The Russian peasant-mother rocks her baby to sleep in a willow basket hung from the ceiling by a stout string.

No. 8. Izba:—A Russian village house.

No. 9. Betrothal Mourning:—The betrothed girl wears mourning because with marriage comes the end of girlhood. The color of the betrothal mourning is blue.

No. 10. The Fast Before Easter:—They give up all animal food, abstaining from meat, and from butter and eggs. In place of butter they use the oil from sunflower seeds during the fasting periods, of which there are several during the year,—seven weeks in Lent, three in June, from the beginning of November until Christmas, and on all Wednesdays and Fridays throughout the year.

No. 11. Bazaar:—A market or shopping place.

No. 12. Tsarskoe Seloe:—More often spelled Tzarskoe Selo, means royal village. As in the case of many other Russian words it is spelled in a variety of ways.

No. 13. Rouble:—A coin worth about fifty cents.

No. 14. Kopeck:—A copper coin worth less than a cent.

No. 15. Troika:—A team of three horses abreast.

No. 16. Tarantas:—A two-seated carriage without springs.

No. 17. Kiosk:—An open summer-house or pavilion.

No. 18. Hussars:—Hussars are horse-soldiers, cavalrymen, who dress in fantastic style. Their uniforms are brilliant in coloring, elaborately braided. The word Hussar is from the Hungarian huszar, meaning twentieth. The original Hussars were Hungarians, one man being chosen out of twenty in each village, to make up the corps. In Russia there are two regiments of Hussars, one red and one green.

No. 19. Moscow:—This city takes its name from the river Moskoa on which it is built. It was formerly the capital of Russia, and is still the most dearly beloved city in the Empire. The people call it the Heart of Russia. Years ago when the French army under Napoleon marched upon it, the citizens, having removed all the relics and household goods possible, set it on fire in eleven places rather than have it fall into the hands of the enemy. As all apparatus for extinguishing the fires had been removed, it burned for three days and three nights, and finally Napoleon and his army were forced to leave it. Its greatest building is the Kremlin, the palace in which the Czars formerly lived. Nobody knows the meaning of the word. This great building stands in the middle of the city and is most imposing.

No. 20. The Mother of Peter the Great was Natalia: —She was the second wife of his father, the

Emperor Alexis. Before the reign of Natalia the women of Russia were not allowed to take part in the daily lives and conversation of the men. But Natalia had been brought up by an uncle who had married a Scotch woman, and she had seen her aunt treated with about the same respect as men were accorded. This seemed right and proper to Natalia, who immediately after her marriage astonished Moscow by driving through the streets with the curtains of her litter undrawn, allowing her face to be seen. She also took part in a series of little plays taken from Scripture, and scandalized the Court by taking an active part in the conversation at formal dinners. It was from his mother that Peter inherited his progressive tendencies.

No. 21. Two Marks:—About fifty cents.

No. 22. Ikon:—A sacred image.

No. 23. Zakuska:—This word means a taste—a little meal. The Russian zakuska consists of highly seasoned food served on the daintiest china the house affords, and eaten standing before the regular meal begins. It is supposed to give one a fine appetite for the heavier food that follows. It consists of raw fish or young pig, very well peppered and cut into small cubes; radishes, olives, pickles, cheese, smoked goose, caviar (smoked or fresh), onions, etc. In poor families the zakuska is simple, consisting usually of pickled suckling pig or fish.

No. 24. Villikens and his Dinah:—Miss Eager, who lived in the Czar's family for six years, frequently sang this song to the children.

No. 25. 8000 roubles:—$4000.00.

No. 26. The Czardas or Csardas:—It is danced with arms folded, the elbows raised to the level of the shoulders. It begins with a sort of heel and toe movement, then follows a glide to right and then to left bringing the feet together after each slide with a snap and at once changing the weight and extending one leg. During the latter hops and slides one hand is at the waist, the other curved diagonally upward. As the dance progresses the stamping of the feet becomes very snappy, and the dancers whirl and turn, always keeping their faces to the front, and striking their heels sharply together, hopping first to one side and then to another, covering as much distance as possible at each hop. Meantime the music is played more and more rapidly. The dance has military dash and precision.

No. 27. The Komarinskaia:—This dance is composed of an unlimited number of steps from which the dancer chooses what he can. The steps call for great strength and agility and usually only men can do them all, although some of the famous Russian dancers who have attended the Imperial Ballet school seem to accomplish them with great ease. In this dance there is even more stamping of the feet than in the Czardas, the knees are frequently bent and the dancer sits almost on his heels, extending one foot and then the other, springing straight up from the heels to a wide, striding position, in which the entire weight of the body falls on the heels. In the dance they slide and stamp, whirl and shout, until the lookers-on shout their bravoes.

No 28. The Polonaise:—A Russian dance (it originated in Poland) consisting mainly of a march of the dancers in procession. It is stately and slow and is in great favor at Imperial balls.

No. 29. Caftans:—Coats worn by Russian coachmen.

No. 30. Revolutionist:—A political term signifying one who is dissatisfied with the government of his country and wishes to overthrow it. George Washington and the leaders of our War for Independence were revolutionists. They were dissatisfied with the way King George III ruled his American Colonies, and they arose in revolt against England and established the Republic of the United States of America. In Russia the revolutionists wish to overthrow the despotic government of the Czar.

NEITHER THE MAN NOR THE CHILD NOTICED THAT A WOMAN
HAD STOPPED IN THE DOORWAY TO WATCH KATRINKA

HER HEART'S DESIRE

Printed in Great Britain
by Amazon

43408940R00199